Millie or Lily?

M. J. Wright

Michelle Wright

First edition

ISBN: 978-0-994648-14-3

A catalogue record for this
book is available from the
National Library of Australia

Other works by M. J. Wright

The Broken Child
The Lost Child

I appreciate everyone who has read this book over the past year. My family who put up with the weirdness of July 2017 when I was supposedly on hiatus from writing-I love you both. My beta readers-Kathy, Angel, Lorna and Jessie. These ladies are awesome. The real location where part of my book has been set. The Lakeside Village Tavern in Raymond Terrace, New South Wales Australia. This place is real. They serve a mean hot chocolate and if you're lucky you might catch me in the corner of the bistro writing.

Table of Contents

As a thin line of orange breaks across the horizon camera flashes reflect off the surface of the cavalcade of all wheel drive vehicles exiting through the gates of Diamond Court, the private community that guaranteed breathing space for the rich and infamous. Lily la Croix observed them through tinted glass, bleary eyes and the steam rising from her cup of coffee.

Running a jaundiced eye over my crazy schedule I took a measured sip of coffee. Vibrations emanating from my phone. Pressing a key with a manicured nail, 'Good morning.' 'Is it?' My brother sounded as if he hadn't turned his coffee machine on yet, 'How crazy is your schedule today?' 'Freaks and geeks on display brother mine.' His laughter echoed down the line. I blew hair out of my face with a puff of breath, 'This is crazy Nick. How am I meant to get behind promoting a book I'm not even finished with yet?' I shot him my schedule for the next few days with a tap of my finger on the screen. His muffled swearing answered my questions for me.

'Who gave the go ahead for half of this stuff?' He asked rhetorically before adding, '4 hours of sleep a night just isn't realistic. You may be the Lily la Croix, but they tend to forget you're only nineteen not a side show pony turning tricks to make them money.' 'What do I do Nick? I'm locked into the contract with almost no wiggle room until the end of this book. The parents refuse to get the lawyers to look over it again even if I pay for it.' A solitary tear rolled down my cheek. Ducking my head so I didn't display my emotions to my driver discreetly wiping it away while taking another sip of coffee. 'Stop crying. I've got the morning free. Let me see what can be arranged. You've still got Oliver Green breathing down your neck correct?' His calm voice soothed my jangled nerves. Coffee wasn't the best thing for me to drink.

'Yes.' Somehow, he knew my entire daily schedule before I did. Used to being constantly on display, I found his tactics for getting photos incredibly invasive. 'I need to disappear to get this book done. There should almost be enough interviews recorded to keep the interest flowing. Tell them I don't want to write any more if something isn't done.' Uttering the words lightens my soul. I'd been hiding my true feelings for a very long time. The car slows at a red light. 'I'll get you the space you need to breathe for a while.' He promises and adds, 'I'll call when I've got news.' 'Okay.' Hanging up the call I finish my drink and prepare for my first interview of the day.

The soft sounds of my writing play list floated softly through my apartment. The change of song disturbed my flow of words. Pulling me away from the train of thought I had been following as my mood swung. I had another thousand words to produce before my afternoon appointment with my editorial team. The monsters in my head were becoming all too real. Something had to give. I needed help for the first time in six years. I couldn't make my characters 'speak' to me. They didn't want the ride to end any more than I did. Lilac Cove had been my entire life for the last six years.

Giving up going to school had been easy. Balancing writing and independent school had been hard. I didn't have close friends. I didn't have any school clubs I was involved in. Boys hadn't even been on my radar. I dreamed, and I wrote. Because of my age I had allowed my parents to convince me to write under a pseudonym. Now I had to embody the pseudonym to the point where even my family forgot that I legally had another name. Staring at the blinking cursor on my monitor I saved my work knowing it would be impossible to slip back into the flow. Maybe this work was meant to be beautifully unfinished.

Two hours later…

'You're short by a chapter.' Flinching internally at the tone in Julie's voice I wait silently for the rant I know is going to follow her opening statement. 'I…' Her words die in her throat when Nick cuts in smoothly, 'Lily is short by a chapter because she has been doing the interview show circuit for the last two weeks. She is up at 3.30 am 5 days a week and most nights doesn't get to bed until after midnight. Now might be a good time to discuss how you plan for her to finish the series?' Hiding my smile, I watch Julie turn red then white then blush a delicate shade of pink. Taking the opportunity to keep talking Nick continues, 'Look at her. Really look at her. She has been writing this series for six years. Churning out a book a year. Neglecting to eat, sleep and have an actual life. Her sacrifices...'

'Her sacrifices are what has made her name so big in such a short space of time.' Julie bristles back. Her ice queen composure locked back into place. 'Yes it has made her a name for herself. So it stands to reason that even big names need to hide from the world to balance out the craziness.' Nick argues back not raising his voice before pointing out, 'I actually have a solution if you'd care to hear it. If you don't then I can pull out the contract and this meeting can get less friendly.'

'I'll hear you out before we make the final decision.' She spits the words at him like darts looking to find a weakness in her enemy's armour. 'You'll hear him out and we'll make the final decision together.' I remind her of her place politely, 'Nick is here because I asked him for help.' She huffs silently before turning her attention to my brother. I just hope that she doesn't lose concentration this time. My very single brother does not need to be dating someone with her attitude. 'Lily will go undercover at my old college. They're looking for someone to run a basic writing course in conjunction with the arts degrees for those who need to catch up. She'd be a student teacher.'

'What would I be studying?' He's put more than a little thought into this. I can teach basic writing 101 in my sleep. 'You my dear sister will be studying life around you. Experiencing things you missed out on in high school. Your cover story is that you're an English major with a minor in Archaeology. You would have to show up to those classes occasionally to make the cover story work.' A grin spreads across my face. A real smile for the first time in months.

CHAPTER ONE

Demons

(Josh)

The lens of the camera could be a magical thing. It shone the spotlight of life on someone else allowing me to hide in the shadows to heal. She was never far from my thoughts. My little girl. My Clarity. Tossing a basketball up in the air I caught it with ease.

All I had of her were the infrequent photographs that his mother dropped off every time they came by to squeeze me for more money. I had been squeezed out of her life before I even knew what was happening. She called my brother 'Daddy' and according to the lawyer I had spoken to I didn't have a legal leg to stand on. My name wasn't on Clarity's birth certificate. Looking at the last one I had been sent on my phone. I couldn't help but smile. She might be the only good thing that happened out of those years. Graduating High School had been hard enough.

Clicking heels across the basketball court from behind me caught my attention. Bloody Norah always catching me in my rare good moments. 'What do you want Norah?' I was tired of her constant games. 'How did you know it was me?' She asked quietly. 'Campus is quiet when school's out.' I repeated my question without turning around, 'What do you want?' We had never had great communication. She was a bottle blond who had started hanging around every time Jed and I worked on the old Charger together.

'Money.' Her voice was hard and flat. 'You have Jed for money.' I tossed the ball at the hoop before facing her, 'Does my forehead have a sign reading ATM?' Her eyes flicked over my outfit before she shrugged one shoulder, 'What do you want me to do? We're both working rotation shifts at the club. Making ends meet and making sure Clarity has her needs covered is hard.' Internally flinching at the slight whine in her voice I shook my head before digging for my last fifty, 'Got nothing left to give. If you want me to keep contributing, you must give us visitation. I want one weekend a month. I'll spend it at Dad's place, so she won't be in the dorms.'

Her green eyes were locked on the crumpled note in my fingers. 'Deal.' She agreed. Smirking I withdrew the paperwork I always carried in my backpack. 'Sign everywhere there's an x. Make sure you get them all Norah. All of them or I'll put the fifty away.' The price of time with my baby girl. Fifty dollars and a well-placed ambush. She used my back as a flat surface.

Checking the paper work I separated the copies and handed her one. 'There'll be a copy filed on Monday. Legal. Watertight. Classes don't start until next month. Plenty of time to squeeze a visit in beforehand.' Her hands shook as she plucked the money from my fist, 'Next Friday.' She agreed, 'Jed will bring her. Your mother wants to talk to you.' 'Not interested.' Was all I tossed into the silence. Norah nodded before clicking her heels across the court back to wherever the hell she came from.

My mother. The woman who had torn our family apart. Not content to be a professor's wife and mother she had invested the family savings into a club downtown. A club that had become the place to pick up your choice of party drugs. Yeah, I didn't need to talk to her again. Thunder sounded off in the distance followed by a flash of lightning. A storm was coming.

Making it home before the storm hit, Dad met me in the kitchen. He was stirring his coffee absentmindedly. 'I got her to sign the papers.' Grabbing a bottle of water from the fridge I asked, 'We've still got all the baby stuff in the attic, don't we?' 'Clarity's coming here.' A smile stretched across his face. 'Next weekend. Friday through to Sunday.' Gulping down the water I caught the goofy look that crossed his face, 'Hold that thought Grandpa. We got some work to do setting up the spare room first.' 'And baby proofing the house.' He agreed. 'Toddler proofing.' I corrected him.

A few weeks later…

'I have a job for you this year.' Direct as always Dad stood in my doorway watching me shove my clean washing into my duffel bag. I had no problem coming home to do laundry when home was a mere stroll across campus.

'Will I be paid?' I asked jokingly. 'I need you to be serious about this Josh.' Dad shoved a hand through his already messy silver streaked hair, 'Please hear me out before responding. I need you to keep an eye on a student teacher. She will be teaching class three nights a week between 10 and 11 in the Creative Arts annex. She's the youngest student teacher we've ever had. She's a big name.'

My ears perked up, 'How big of a name?' Like all photographers dreaming of signing onto a magazine I wanted that one golden money shot. 'No photos.' Dad stipulated before chucking my Dr Who shirt across the room at me. 'Who?' catching the shirt one handed I waited. 'Lily la Croix.'

'Lily la Croix.' A slow grin spread across my face. The ice princess of the press. Darling of the public. 'No photos.' Dad reiterated before adding, 'She'll be here in disguise. Millie has exclusive access to the tunnels from Black House.'

She had the biggest single on campus. The last student who had lived in that suite had been royalty from one of the Arabic countries. 'She's here to finish her book. Can you please make sure no one bothers her?' Dad looked exhausted, 'Her agent has been quite verbal about her security.'

I slung my bag over my shoulder, 'When should I expect her?' There was no use arguing with him over something as trivial as making sure the princess got to and from class alright. 'Tonight.' Dad grabbed me in a hug before stepping back, 'See you next weekend for Sunday Dinner?' I smirked at him, 'Free food. I'll let you know who else is coming.'

CHAPTER TWO

Late Night Arrival

There was something about the angles of the buildings on campus at night. The different play of light and shade brought out a darker shade of beauty in my photos. A beat up crummydore rolled up into the empty parking lot disturbing the serene atmosphere.

She had been on the news only a few hours ago describing the latest addition in her break out book series. Anyone who had a pulse had heard of Lilac Cove. All the girls loved the romance and the hot guys. All the guys drooled over the chicks on the covers. I studied her through the lens of my camera. Her polish had long since been smudged.

Wearing a somewhat stylish red coat paired with some comfortable denim jeans most of her flawless white skin was hidden from view. Black large framed geek glasses covered her face and her previously styled hair flowed loose over her shoulders. The guy she was with wore the same style glasses. There was enough of a family resemblance for me to assume that the guy shadowing her was her brother Nick. He shouldered her frayed back pack and hefted a matching duffel bag. I had thought she would have rolled up in her Shelby Cobra GT500 or at the very least in her Ford Mondeo. Enough students around here were rich enough to travel in style so she would have fit right in.

Shouldering her tote and shoving her hands in her front pockets I could tell she was shivering even from this distance. A light breeze sent a chill down my own back.

Dad and I had come to an arrangement. I would watch over little miss superstar in exchange for a place to go with Clarity on my weekends with her, ongoing tuition support for my double degrees of photography and business.

Everyone was worth at least one photo and fifteen minutes of fame. Even though the exquisite creature in the parking lot was pretending to be ordinary the camera loved her. There was something about her face. A wary kind of innocence. Keeping my lens hidden from the light I snapped a quick close up of the apprehension expressed on it plainly for the world to see. Nick gestured to her before the tail lights on the commodore flashed once signalling that he had locked it. They set off at a slow stroll on the path that would lead them directly to the nearest tunnel door.

Leaning against the cement pillar I began to review my work for the night. Classes were due to begin in the next couple of days. My life was already messy enough. I was extremely busy trying to carry my course loads and then there was Clarity. I didn't have time for any distractions. I had a feeling the ice princess would be a major one if I let her under my skin.

Waiting until I could no longer see shapes on the path I slung my camera over my shoulder and withdrew my pack of cigarettes from my back pocket. Attempting to cut back now that Clarity was in my life I was down to two a day. Blowing smoke into the air I nodded to the night security guard. I was on first names with most of them since I lived on campus year-round. Finishing the cigarette quickly I disposed of it before making my own way back to the dorms.

Ryan my roommate wasn't due to arrive until the first day of classes. His grandmother needed treatment in the hospital and the whole family had put their lives on hold to be with her. 'You the one watching her?' The question caught me unaware. Nick st James had a no-nonsense air about him. He crossed his arms clearly waiting for my answer. 'Josh Patterson.' Introducing myself I held my hand out to him. He had a firm grasp. 'The professor's kid, right?' His stern demeanour broke into an easy grin. 'Yeah that's me.' My tone conveying how thrilled I was with his description. 'Didn't mean any disrespect. I know how life gets around here. She'll miss it all unless you give her a little nudge to go to at least one party. I want her to do what she came to do but I also want her to learn how to live outside of her own head.' He held out a business card to me. 'What's this?' I knew what it was, but I needed to hear it from him. 'Her number. I'm not setting her up for failure. Use it to get her out of her shell.' He sized me up before adding, 'If you do want time with her do it because she's amazing not because she'll make you famous. Lily's been used too many times to jump start other people's careers. She won't survive another heartache like that.'

His phone vibrated in his hand. 'That's her.' He looked up at me, 'Keep my sister safe.' He tapped a message on his keypad before striding back across campus to his car.

CHAPTER THREE

Alias

(Millie)

Leaning my head against the cold glass of the window I lose myself in the swirling thoughts inside my head. Struggling to finish the seventh book in the Lilac Cove series, everyone decided that I would benefit from a drop of normalcy in my life. Normal. I tried that once. Before life got crazy. Before I lived a fish bowl existence of a life.

Julie finally agreed to follow through with Nick's idea. She approached the college with a deal they couldn't refuse. Damn savvy publishing house rep. She insists that I go to college for the full experience since I missed out on the testing grounds of high school. Her words not mine. My memories of high school were one of a daily hellish existence. I remember hiding away in corners scribbling stories on spare scraps of paper until one day I stuffed the completed manuscript in an envelope and mailed it to a slush pile.

Sighing softly, briefly wondering why this book is taking forever to finish I attempt to get more comfortable against the cold pane of glass. I've already taken the advance royalties. I feel so out of touch with my peers but then again, I've always felt out of step with people my own age. Classes start in less then 2 days. I don't have time for college. Was I crazy to agree to pretend to be a mousy student teaching creative writing for dummies? Why did I agree to find out what I'm missing out on?

'Doing okay over there?' Nick asks breaking the silence in the car. 'Nervous.' I reply softly. There's not enough caffeine in the world to prepare someone for leaving home for the first time. 'You know I wouldn't have suggested this plan if I didn't think it was something you could benefit from.' He pulls up at a red light and turns to me taking the few minutes to assess my condition, 'You'll be fine.'

Sneaking me onto campus in the middle of the night he grins at me, 'Want to have some fun?' He turns up a street full of mid-century modern houses. One of the houses has a black Challenger in the driveway. Nick's smile widens as if he knows the owner of the car. 'This is professor row.' He revs the commodore's engine before executing two perfect donuts and accelerating away from the scene of the crime.

Raising my eyebrow, I wait for an explanation. 'I was part of the underground car racing circuit while I was here.' He confesses, 'It was a big part of my study hard and play harder persona.' He pulls into an empty parking lot. 'Right. This is the building where you'll spend your time teaching. Your classes finish at 11. So you need to get used to walking across campus at this time of night.'

Nick slips on the same thick frame nerd glasses I prefer to wear when no one else can see me. Loading up with my belongs he gives me a moment to scan my new surroundings.

Huffing slightly to keep up with his long strides he stops and peers down at me concerned. 'Inhaler?' he demands. I wave it at him before taking my medication. Geek glasses and inhalers don't quite go with the ice princess persona I've built up with the media. Heaven forbid they should actually find out that I practically live in comfy flannelette shirts, jeans, and my favourite worn uggs while I'm working. Slipping the inhaler into the pocket of my jacket we resume walking through the crisp night.

We arrive at the red wooden door barely visible in the wall of overgrown greenery. Making sure we aren't being observed first Nick takes out an old lace wrought iron key from the dark ages. It's a pretty piece of ephemera that does not belong is this modern world. Automatic lighting flickers on as we set foot into the tunnels. I know what you're thinking either this college has had tons of secret societies or my security team is way over the top in ensuring my safety at all times. The whole campus is riddled with them. No one knows why they were built only that they're here and mine allows me to go three places without stepping foot into the hallway of the main dorm.

Just because I agreed to this experiment didn't mean I want to be mobbed every time I leave my room. Call it a compromise. Those tunnels are my freedom in a world full of crazy fans. When I first created Lilac Cove I didn't expect the world to go gaga for Missy and Dan. Now

I'm on the seventh book in the series I can't seem to say goodbye.

He drops my bags unceremoniously on the floor in the spacious suite of rooms I'll be living out of for the next year. Nick pokes his head into the bathroom making sure no one is hiding out in there before wrapping me up in the best brother's hug ever. He pulls back before saying, 'Guess this is it, kid.' He doesn't tell me how proud he is of me for taking such a giant step or any of the other platitudes family throw out when a child leaves the nest for the first time.

'Guess so.' The moroseness of my mood seeps into the tone of my voice. I don't get lonely but I don't want to live a gazillion miles away from Nick either. 'Cheer up. Live a little. Make Millie work for you.' Nick heads back towards the door on the far wall concealing the tunnels. I nod jumping slightly at the door banging shut somewhere else in the building.

Millie. My alter ego. She's a no one from nowhere and she teaches creative writing for dummies. That's not what the college is calling the course but it's what I'm calling it in my head. I created Millie. She's mine not some product of my media manager's. Sue is an absolute shark when comes to being the queen of spin. I only agreed because they'd let me come up with my alter ego.

Millie (no last name). That's who I am for three nights a week between 8 pm and 11 at night. Millie is a brunette. I'm a blonde. Her hair is wavy and mine is sleekly styled. She dresses romantic bohemian. I'm more classic in style. Unless I'm writing and then grunge could set up a postcode all of its own in my office.

Millie is shy. Sits on the fringes of society and doesn't make friends easily. She's kind and gentle. The core part of the Millie identity. The important part. This is when there is no dividing line between Millie or Lily. At the heart, we're the same person.

I've seen the pictures in the file of my suite. It's just like any other luxurious hotel room with a large sitting area, a comfortable workstation, plush size king bed and a table for two for eating at. Food will be delivered in the hours I'm at work so that my kitchen is kept fully stocked.

There's no television. There never is. Television is just an excuse to be distracted by the noise of life. I can stream news, Spotify, and Netflix if I want to be entertained. I pull out my phone and text Nick.

I don't know where any of my clothes are ???

In the panels behind your bed. There's nothing for you to 'do' and nowhere you need to 'be' until Monday night. Sue left your disguise in the bathroom in case you want to check out the campus.

You shouldn't text and drive.

I'm not :p Still sitting in the car. Knew you'd need me.

Go home big bro. Love you. Call on Sunday yeah?

Ok :)

CHAPTER FOUR

The Garden Café

Coffee! I need coffee to dispel the gloom of the minimalist atmosphere the decorators of this suite seem to love. Clean lines with a palette of grey, black and slightly warm white is definitely not my thing. Thank all of creation that they redesigned my writing area so that I could function correctly.

I still needed to find where they were hiding my breakfast foods. Stumbling over to the kitchenette I open the fridge door.

None of the contents are drawing my eye. A bright yellow post it note grabs my attention from its position on the egg carton.

Microwave oats in pantry.3rd cupboard to the left. You also have chocolate up and go on the top shelf.

Mum

Makes sense that Mum organised the groceries and layout. She knows that I don't eat well until about lunchtime…if I remember lunch at all. Shutting the fridge door I rummage through all of the cupboards. No coffee machine? No caffeine in any form at all? This isn't going to work.

Ambling slowly toward the bathroom squinting against the bright sunbeams bursting merrily through the glass wall I snag the clothes I picked out before bed as I pass the timber clothes valet. Sighing softly in appreciation at the underfloor heating in the bathroom I dump my belongings unceremoniously on the long bench beside the makeup counter. Everything was laid out neatly for my transformation from myself into Millie included another colour coded post it note with instructions reminding me to keep my makeup minimal and natural.

Yellow for family, purple for my stylist, blue for the cleaning service and white for Julie. As if I couldn't remember simple instructions for brush through colour and new contacts. Flipping the light switch, I'm blinded by the instant flickering flame in the fireplace and the multi wattage bursting from the chandelier above me. Taking the opportunity to time the whole transformation process I start with a shower and move onto to hair and makeup. Unfamiliar grey eyes stare back at me from the strange reflection in the mirror.

Stepping out into the garden alley a good while later wearing a Millie approved outfit consisting of a soft pink turtleneck paired with jeans, chunky boots and a black anorak. I clutch at my triquetra pendant for luck before slipping the Celtic turquoise ring Nick gave me on the pinkie finger of my left hand. I needed to find caffeine, so I could knock out a few chapters around what was left of my unpacking.

Locking the door carefully behind me I followed the path that meandered around through the overgrown garden. Just set off the herringbone brickwork were two red iron chairs with a small table between them. The half-hidden shop front had an old English charm with a slightly neglected air.

'Please tell me you've come for coffee and some breakfast. Not the charm and the free Wi-Fi.' She looked out of place behind the counter. This girl had an overall edgy feel to her personality. 'I'll take a Chai latte with two sugars. What's good on the breakfast menu?' Holding her gaze with a shy smile it takes me a split second to remember that I'm not supposed to be this confident. 'Call me Emerson. Our waffles are good, but you look like someone who appreciates pancakes or a breakky wrap.'

An easy choice. 'Pancakes please no ice cream.' Taking a look around the empty Café I chose a corner booth diagonal to the entry. Enjoying the atmosphere of the quaint little coffee shop it isn't long before Emerson places a plate in front of me and returns with a tall steaming mug. 'Emerson as in the famous Author?' I couldn't help but ask. 'No Emerson the botanist. He discovered some aquatic fungus family that made him wiki famous. My mum has a thing for gardening.' She slid into the booth opposite me, 'I haven't seen you around before. Are you a new transfer?'

'Something like that.' I cage taking a bite of the pancakes off the end of my fork. 'Something like that or exactly like that?' She challenges sounding more bitter then sarcastic. 'I'm not a transfer. I'm here to eat and recaffienate.' Taking another bite of the pancakes and a swallow of coffee I eye her warily over the edge of the coffee mug. Her attitude had grated on my already raw nerves and the clock hadn't even struck nine yet. 'I'm a new student teacher.' I admit with a nervous laugh tossing her a bone to keep the conversation going.

Pushing a hand through her granny dyed dark hair she scans my face critically before commenting, 'Aren't you a little young to be a student teacher?' Smiling cryptically around the coffee mug I watch as she subsides a little. I didn't care if people thought I was too young.

'It's what I am.' I state calmer now the caffeine was mixing with my bloodstream, 'I'm Millie.' 'Emmie' she offers dropping the bitch act, 'I don't normally take the morning shift. Too early for me. Sometimes I can't pass up the money though.' 'I hear that. I'm working the late shift when I'd rather be chilling with pizza and a movie.' Shyly offering my own opinion she breaks out into a genuine smile,

'Don't be a stranger Millie. I'm good for advice, fashion tips, awesome coffee and cute guy alerts.'

CHAPTER FIVE

First Class

(Millie)

Entering a cavernous lecture hall my eyes sweep over row upon row of empty chairs. Of course, no one came. Everyone had something else they would rather be doing at night then attending a optional class entitled blandly 'Chats with Millie'. I'd heard it being referred to as 'creative writing for dummies 101' half a dozen times in the last two days when I'd been on a hunt for great coffee. The buzz surrounding the class had been that the administration had initially made the class mandatory and then backed down after a student uproar.

Staring around the empty seats once more with a sinking heart, I put away the usb containing the PowerPoint presentation I had prepared and put my bag down on the lecturer's desk. Opening the screen up on my laptop I ignore the Doctor Who episode I have on pause on Netflix and hover my mouse over Scrivener instead.

He hadn't turned up to meet her. Their shady little grotto felt empty without him.

Setting up a timer on my phone I continue to tap out a mundane little scene showing the cracks forming between Missy and Dan's relationship. High school was long over for these two and the love affair I had once held with their dream romance was long over for me too. Leaning back in the chair rotating my shoulders to stretch out the muscles I wonder which ending Julie would end up accepting.

If I wanted to be completely honest with myself and everyone around me Missy jilted Dan at the altar. She felt that she was too young to know what she wanted from life. That ending was already written leaving the reader with a hint of more possibly in ten years' time when I didn't feel so jaded. I just needed another alternative second half of the manuscript that left everything completed. People wanted a light hearted, feel good story when it came to Lilac Cove. They didn't want the story whisking them away from their real world to mirror it in the harsh reality of daylight and coffee.

Coffee. Taking a sip from my travel mug I can almost feel it working its magic around my veins. Enlivening me so that I can keep working. Before I can keep typing my alarm echoes through the empty building. Turning it off quickly, I save my work and slide my laptop back into my shoulder bag. Sighing deeply, I allow my eyes to slide around the room again. I hope this wasn't going to be a regular occurrence.

Despite the whole alias thing I was actually looking forward to sharing my knowledge with a new crop of upcoming writers. Tonight's vote of no confidence left me feeling more like a failure than ever.

Locking the door, I wander down the long hall taking my time. Everywhere I look there is bright colours. Plush stuffed bench seats are pushed back against tall windows in the foyer. An empty coffee cart stands waiting for the morning stampede in one corner. A reception area in the other. Sighing in slight regret I push the outer door open and step into the cool night air before turning to lock it as well.

The harsh overhead florescent lighting reflected off a surface causing me to instinctively duck my head away from a possible lens. Light glinting off glass. Instant giveaway. Amateur. A small smile curls my lips upward slightly. I normally wouldn't turn away so quickly. Millie is supposed to be camera shy. Hates having her photo taken. Raising my head so that a sheet of hair separates me from the unwanted intrusion I keep moving forward. Right into a hard body. The distinct scent of leather and aftershave curl its way into my nostrils. Gentle hands help steady me on my feet.

'I'm sorry.' The apology automatically falls from my lips. 'My bad.' His voice is smooth with a hint of laughter, 'Camera shy?' 'It's not pointed at me right now is it?' I ask his black boots. They look comfortable. 'So not the time to be thinking this.' I chastise myself silently while I wait for an answer. 'Nope.' He pops the p. A small giggle escapes before I can hold it in. Damn. I'm not a giggler. Especially not when a hot guy is staring down at me in concern. His blue eyes are an unusual shade.

'Camera Boy.' I greet him with a smile. 'Writer Girl.' He shoots back at me easily running a hand through the bleached top of his blond/brunette hair. Another odd feature. His parents must be supermodels or something. 'Didn't scare you too badly did I?' He asks. Shaking my head silently I drop the keys to the building inside my jacket pocket. 'I don't like having my photo taken.' I explain softly. The campus is peaceful at this time of night. Serene even if the lights weren't making that infernal buzzing noise. Maintenance really needed to step up their game.

'I'll remember that.' He slings his camera over his shoulder with ease, 'Got far to go?' Cocking an eyebrow at him I wait for an explanation. 'Stranger danger and all that.' He slides a beanie on his head and pulls it down to cover his ears. 'You're a stranger to me.' I point out the fact, 'I'm hardly going to give away information on where I live am I?'

Tyres screaming against asphalt destroys the peacefulness we have created between us. Whoever is driving doesn't give two shits about their engine. His body posture changes as a black challenger pulls up with a screech. Turning to conceal my presence he sweeps me behind him gently, 'If I say lock yourself inside the building don't stop to ask questions alright?'

He looks back over his shoulder to check if I understand his strange request. Nodding slightly, I can't help myself, 'Friends of yours?' Doors opening. Two of them. 'I'll explain later. I say run. You run and lock yourself in.' He repeats himself before turning to face whomever it is that has put him on edge. Peeking out from behind his broad shoulders I silently memorise the number plate. Connecting the dots swiftly in my head I realise that this is the car that set Nick off the other night.

CHAPTER SIX

Unpleasant Experience

(Josh)

She looks up at me like a little kitten bristling with false courage. I can tell she's curious but trusts me to handle the situation. Fully clad in leather they make their way towards us under the bright sensor lights at the entrance of the building. Heels on the pavement clicking against my fraying temper. He's my brother. Bloody Norah. Mother of my child dragging my brother Jed along with her. Drunk as usual or high or both.

I can smell the alcohol fumes pouring off them. If I lit a match and tossed it at them I bet they'd both go down in a blaze of…well it definitely wouldn't be glory. Taking off my camera I hand it to the silent girl I was sheltering behind me. Out of sight out of mind. I couldn't afford to replace the one thing that had kept me sane these last few years.

Delicate fingers touch my hand in reassurance before letting go. 'Jed. Norah.' My voice is neutral. My face blank. Untouchable. 'Kid.' Jed greets me. It's been six months since I last saw him. 'Mum sends her regards.' He rasps out. Norah clings to him tightly.

Narrowing my eyes, I point at him with an unlit cigarette, 'I'll bet she does. I'm not coming to work at the bar for her. You're wasting your time as usual. Dad's got Clarity at the house.' His hands double up into fists. Norah whispers into his ear pouring her sweet poison through him as always.

'Who are you hiding?' She asks me hearing Millie's fidgeting behind me. 'No one you need to know.' I counter. Millie touches the back of my jacket. She's tapping out a message in Morse code.

They're dragging this out for a reason. Hiding something of their own.

Looking quickly over my shoulder she gives me a determined nod. 'Ask what they're hiding.' She mouths at me. Damn she's good. I wonder how long she's been profiling people. 'You're holding me here. Any reason why?' Directing my question to Jed I begin to back Millie closer to the building. 'Mum decided to pay Dad a visit.' He replies nonchantly.

Mum decided to pay Dad a visit at the house. *Clarity's at the house.* He started this mess with Mum he could deal with her but heaven help her if there was even a scratch on Clarity's skin. 'Why keep me here?' Another two steps backwards.

She's moving fluidly in sync with me. 'I wanted to see you.' He admits quietly. My brother wanted to spend time with me. I light my cigarette. Deliberately taking my time before exhaling in their direction, 'You want to see me. Come in daylight. Leave the eye candy behind. Come sober and call in advance. I may have a class.'

'Who're you calling eye candy?' Norah snarls. 'He didn't mean it that way babe.' Jed tries to appease her before the situation escalates beyond our control. 'He did mean it.' She argues back slurring her words slightly before zeroing in on trying to see around me to catch a glimpse of Millie. Nope. Not happening. Another two steps backwards. 'Get inside and lock the door until I tell you it's okay.' I throw over my shoulder. Keys jangling as she searches for the exact one she needs. Feeling the breeze at my back and hearing a slight click I relax slightly knowing that she's safe.

'What have you taken?' Jed doesn't look so good. His skin tone has a weird ashy undertone which has never been there before. 'Just something to help us feel good. You're being the responsible one tonight.' Norah laughs her mood swings giving me whiplash as I try to catch up. Shaking my head, I know better than to try to appeal to her when she's in this state. A blast of sixxam echoes out before Jed pulls out his phone. He listens for a couple of minutes before hanging up. 'We gotta bounce babe.' He tugs on Norah's arm to grab her attention before promising quietly, 'I'll be seeing you Josh.'

I don't move until the challenger peals away from the parking lot. I spent years working on that car with him. Shaking away the memories I turn to face the girl half masked by shadows on the other side of the window pane. Visible relief etched in the fine lines stand out in sharp contrast against the pale skin of her face.

Double checking that the building is secure yet again she joins me leaning against another side of the square cement post. Waiting patiently for me to finish the cigarette she angles herself upwind of the smoke. 'Questions?' the word drops out of my mouth sarcastically before I can reel both it and my poor mood in. 'Would you mind walking me across campus?' Her next words surprise me, 'Somehow I feel safer when you're with me.' Cradling my camera with care she hands it back to me. 'Not so scary now is it.' cracking the first joke that comes to mind to clear the air of the weird tension between us I catch the small fleeting smile that races across her features. 'Fear of cameras no. Fear of social media more like.' she hastens to explain herself nervously shifting from one foot to the other, 'I live in…' 'Black House.' I finish for her, 'Yeah I've seen you around.'

CHAPTER SEVEN

Writers Block

A/N Josh's texts are in *italics*. Millie's texts are in **bold** and Millie's thoughts are normal text.

(Millie)

I never did get a proper explanation for what happened. It wasn't my business anyway. Students slowly began to trickle into attending my classes. I turned it into a discussion group for the finer points of writing that the mainstream courses tended to skate over.

I only saw camera boy late at night taking photos. Early mornings didn't count. He seemed to have a pretty strong fan base of his own to deal with. While I didn't know the details, I knew what it was like to be hunted. To never have a moment's peace to yourself. To have each minute of every day scheduled.

I would love to say that each time they mobbed him I gracefully juggled both coffees without spilling a drop. Usually the most vocal girl ended up having to rush home after screaming abuse at me.

About a month had passed and I had even persuaded Emerson Rose to come and check out my class. It was free after all. Underneath the sass was an intelligent creative artist waiting to be released.

Staring out my tinted one-way windows at the busy campus I absentmindedly sipped my coffee. I had spent hours with my fingertips paused on the keys of my computer keyboard waiting for inspiration to hit.

Nothing. Nada. Zip. Writers block had hit at the worst possible time.40,000 more words. Happy words. Relationships would work out. All would be right in everyone's universe but mine. Dare I even entertain the thought? I couldn't. I needed to finish both versions of the book. My way and the way I knew they would eventually choose. I didn't feel comfortable in my surroundings. I had that feeling that my skin had somehow shrunk on my body while I wasn't looking.

Not being able to write hurt my soul. I had so much I wanted to tell the world. Not a single word of it transcribed onto the screen. Slamming my laptop shut in frustration I slid it into my bag and grabbed a pair of sunglasses. Leaving my garden tunnel exit was a little trickier during the daytime. Using the camera monitor I made sure the lane way was empty before opening the door.

The warmth of the sun blinded me momentarily. Sliding the blue shades down over my eyes I decided to explore where the lane way ended. Instead of stopping in at the Garden café I kept walking until I found a Narnia like lamp post. A wrought iron beacon against the night terrors. Frustrated with myself my hands tighten into fists. I could think it. I could see the whole scene inside my head but I couldn't put the words down on paper to save myself. Keeping to the right every time the path forked I travel another ten minutes before finding a lonely park bench beside a creek. The water rippled against the stones on the bottom as it ambled past me. Time slowing down creating the bubble of peace I had been desperately seeking.

My phone beeped. Couldn't I have five minutes? Every night after class I found reminder notes from everyone who ran my universe. They needed to see progress. I hadn't been wearing the right outfit. Was I eating? Who was supplying my coffee? An endless rainbow colour of post it notes. My phone beeped again demanding that I pay it attention. Digging the device out of my front pocket I opened the message with a couple of taps to the screen.

Hi :) Is this a bad time?

There was no assigned name. I didn't recognise the phone number. I had been handing it out on my hand outs in class. Tapping out a quick reply I waited to see if the sender would be more forthcoming. Barely 2 seconds passed before the phone warbled the message tone at me again.

I believe you called me Camera Boy.

I hadn't spoken to him since that night he had walked me home across campus. The corners of my mouth tugged upwards at the corners as I tapped my reply out quickly teasing him slightly.

Creepy camera boy who's always stalking my late-night class?

I knew he was keeping some kind of surveillance on me. Why? I wondered briefly if it had anything to do with the mysterious exchange he had had with the strangers in leather. 'Not so strange to him though.' I mused to myself taking a deep cleansing breath.

Creepy? Really? I make sure you get home safe princess.

Oh. That made sense. But I still didn't understand why he had appointed himself my personal guardian. My fingers flew over the tiny keyboard before I gave myself time to question my thoughts.

Why? I mean I guess I should thank you but I don't understand why you'd do that.

My phone beeped almost immediately. Damn the boy must have fingers of fury or something.

Jed and Norah. Mainly Norah. She won't stop until she's caught a glimpse of you. She's high and drunk half the time.

Lovely. I sense a lot of history between you two. Now I'm in the middle of something.

My fingers flew responding with as much implied sarcasm as possible dripping from my every word.

Let me make it up to you then. I noticed you don't go out a lot.

There's a party this weekend at Blue House. Want to hang?

Want to hang? I stifled a laugh. Of course, I wanted to go to a party. I just hadn't gotten the courage up to experience one yet. The fact that he was trying to deflect me away from his business had not been lost on me either. Whatever. It wasn't right for me to pry into something that he clearly wanted me protected from.

What do you say writer girl?

There was really only one answer I could give.

Yes. Aren't you in the middle of Dynamic Accounting now?

Dynamic Accounting?

I could hear the smirk behind the words as the penny dropped that I knew which class he was currently sitting in.

Now who's being creepy ;)

Laughing openly. My bad mood had disappeared completely. I tap out a reply to him before tilting my face to the sun. I didn't see enough of the sky. Squinting up at the wispy clouds floating by, one by one my back muscles relax out of their usual tense state.

I heard one of the barbies going over your schedule this morning.

btw you're welcome for the wasted caffeine.

That's you?

What could I say? I had to keep my caffeine intake on the down low from all the spies Julie had planted everywhere. Hoodies, sunglasses and Uggs were brilliant inventions for travelling incognito.

Yeah. One cup for me and one for the bimbo who can't walk on her own lol.

LMAO who knew you had it in you. This class is drier than the Sahara.

Then why take it?

Obligations. Millie?

Yes Josh?

You intrigue me.

I intrigued him? If anything, he had intrigued me with his carefully cultivated bad boy image. Opening my laptop I began to type for the first time all day.

Taking a sip of my cold coffee I paused to save his number under Camera Boy. He had enough mamma drama that should be sending me running in the opposite direction and yet…there was something about him. Something I couldn't quite put my finger on. Something real.

Once the words began to flow they kept coming. I wrote two chapters before stretching. Shadows were creeping across the grass toward me. Saving my work I packed up for the quick walk back home.

I stopped writing in the early hours of the morning. Once I had started the words wouldn't stop coming. I always experienced the same phenomena. Not being able to write and then having too much to say. Stretching my hands above my head I felt my back crack as something popped back into place.

Humming a random tune to myself I make myself a proper meal for once. Lamb chops with veggies and mashed potato. Cheesy garlic bread on the side. My phone beeps. Camera Boy.

Do you know what time it is?

Not really. I've been binge writing. Y?

It's 2 am writer girl.

:o Late for you then

Normal for you I take it :o

I decide not to shock him even further by admitting that I've just made my dinner.

Is when I'm writing. What made you start texting me?

Besides the fact that you notice everything about everybody?

Not everybody. You know my schedule probably as well as I know yours. Why are you texting me?

I want real answers. He won't answer anything about Jed and Norah. I'm hoping his intentions are good ones.

Direct aren't you.

It's the middle of the night. Words have a power of their own at night :)

True.

He doesn't elaborate further. Thirty minutes passes while I putter around with a cup of tea in my hand to help me wind down. Turning off most of my lights enables me to see the red glow of a cigarette tip in the lane way.

Millie?

Yes Josh.

You don't get enough sleep. Go to bed Princess.

Night.

It was a strange feeling having someone care if I got enough sleep. Saving my work, I powered down the laptop I had resting beside me and slid between the cool sheets in my bed.

CHAPTER EIGHT

Party

Uploading my latest offering to Julie in an effort to appease her I twirled in my chair watching the bar fill with colour showing its progress. One month. They had only given me one lousy month before the whole dog and pony show was threatening to descend on me once again.

My email chimed loudly. Julie.

Great Job. We'll talk Monday when I've read them both.

J.

Great job? What was I? A tween that needed constant congratulations on minor milestones. The party at Blue House didn't officially start for another couple of hours. I had heard that they planned on kicking things off with a barbeque and game of football.

Hearing my phone beep with an incoming text I turn it over to be greeted with a message from camera boy.

Morning :)

Is it? Jk I've been up for a few hours already.

How many words writer girl?

Only a few thousand. All good ones.

Sounds good. See you in a few hours.

I'll be the one wearing heels. :(

Heels? Going all out to impress me huh?

Who says I'm wearing heels to impress you? I might need some makeshift stakes for random vampires.

Cos all the skin bling would be a dead giveaway.

Team Jacob or team Edward? :P

I wondered if my tween obsession reference had been too much in response to his Twilight reference. Too late I'd already sent it.

Josh?

Team Alice ;) Yes Millie.

I'll c u there.

(Josh)

Putting my phone on my bedside table I roll over and smile up at the ceiling. She got me. She got my random references to television shows and movies. She knew when to call me out for pushing the friendship a little too hard. If you could even call what we had a friendship. It was more like a chat thing than anything else.

I didn't have Clarity this weekend. She had begun calling me 'Daddy Josh' so that she didn't confuse me with her other

Daddy. Jed. Scanning the latest photo of us in a frame on my bedside table her infectiousness radiated through the frame at me. Eating ice cream out of a small to go cup it was smeared right across her chubby cheeks.

My thoughts circled back to Millie again. Something about her was beginning to concern me. She practically lived in her dorm like a hermit. Working so intensely around the clock was taking a toll on her. Too much caffeine was making her jumpy.

She needed to break free and have some fun. I knew just the guy to help me. Too bad I would have to wait another hour or so before he woke up.

(Millie)

Sitting in a cane chair placed artfully under a spreading jacaranda tree in the shade, I watched the football game unfold. Teams were formed by just running onto either end of the back yard.

Hot sizzling sounds blended with laughter and back ground music to form a relaxed atmosphere. Taking a breath, I surveyed the crowd around the food table.

I grabbed the same paper plate as someone else. Mortified hot colour stained my cheeks. 'Here.' A friendly voice handed it to me. 'Thanks.' His eyes are light grey with a dark grey rim. Different. I wonder whether I can work that into my book anywhere. 'I don't think I've seen you in any of my classes.' He wipes his hand on his jeans, 'Ryan Western.'

I take it and reply, 'I teach a class three nights a week. I'm Millie.' A slow grin spreads across his face, 'Millie huh? Which subject?' It was refreshing not to hear that I was a little young. 'I teach creative writing for dummies 101.' Loading up my plate I caught the double take out of the corner of my eye. Grabbing a plastic fork and a bottle of water I wait with arched eyebrow.

He rubs the back of his head sheepishly, 'uh yeah. About that. I started calling it that.' Yup. I can totally believe that. He looks like he belongs on the football field rather than indoors creating the next best seller. Light laughter spills from my lips unbidden. 'I'm not offended.'

'You should be.' a curly haired brunette joins us, 'I've sat in on two of your classes. You make our syllabus easy. I'm Cassie.' Cassie sends Ryan a withering look, 'If our mother didn't force us to admit we were siblings I probably wouldn't most of the time. 'Cassie seems down to earth and easy going. We make plans to meet up for coffee before I slip back to the far end of the garden. I'm thankful Nick isn't here to embarrass me in public like that. Cassie is still telling Ryan off about something. I feel like cringing on his behalf.

'I'm so hot I could give the sun a cuddle.' Josh collapses dramatically on the ground beside me. I drop the unopened water bottle beside him. It's still nice and cold. Uncapping it he chugs half of the bottle without taking a break. 'Great line.' I smirked mentally making a note of it, 'Can I steal it?'

'Writer girl.' He grinned, 'How are you enjoying the party?' He takes his time with the other half of the water. 'Incoming!' Football. My face. Not happening. I catch it neatly and get ready to return it. 'Toss it back.' Josh encourages me. Practicing with Nick was about to come in very handy.

A small smile tugs at my lips as I stand and let it soar back through the air. 'Beautiful.' I hear from behind me, 'What other talents are you hiding from the world writer girl?'

He stops speaking. Pointing at me with his forefinger he said, 'You haven't even gone inside and mingled yet have you?' I shrugged. Didn't seem like it was worth my time to be honest. There were half empty cups of beer littering every surface and random strangers were swapping spit with each other. He shook his head and bounced back up onto his feet, 'Sorry writer girl you gotta have the full party experience.'

I knew I was going to regret the decision before I even made it. Grabbing his hand, he helped me up from the ground and led me through the yard towards the thumping bass. Barbeque forgotten. Football game nearly abandoned in favour of dancing and drinking.

Skimpily clad women were rubbing up against anything with a heartbeat inside the main living area which had been turned into a makeshift dance floor. Taking a sealed bottle of water from the tub of half melted ice I watched warily as the women swooped like a flock of birds.

'You didn't tell me that you knew Josh Patterson.' Emerson Rose fanned herself, 'That boy is to die for and worse luck is he knows it.' Emmie was wearing a magenta skin-tight dress that looked incredibly uncomfortable.

'Is that his name? I've always called him camera boy.' I yell in her ear, 'You look amazing.' She takes a better look at my outfit, 'You look like you've come from coffee with your mother. Next time call me before leaving your dorm room.'

I think…in fact I absolutely know that I won't be doing that anytime soon. I've been inside for five minutes and already my anxiety level is rising.

Running a hand through his bleached hair his blue eyes meet mine. Another guy muscles through the crowd to reach his side. 'Alright ladies. My man Josh has asked me to take your credentials to go through at his leisure.' An easy smile lights up the circle of disappointed faces, 'Pass em up so he can be on his way.'

'Ryan. Play nice.' I lip read as Emmie sighs dramatically, 'Josh and Ryan together. My heart can't take it.' 'What's Ryan's story?' I find myself asking before examining the water bottle for puncture marks. Don't ask. I learnt early in my career to be super paranoid when my security wasn't around.

'Josh's bestie, roomie and all-around hottie.' Emmie joins the back of the queue that has formed. Amused I shake my head as she pulls a business card out of the top of her dress.

Another warm body takes her spot against the wall beside me. I glance up. Josh's blue eyes twinkle down at me, 'Want to go?' Go. Yes. I want to leave this crazy experience and never repeat it again.

Outside on the pavement the sudden stillness washes over my soul. One cold wet drop hits my bare shoulder. Lightning snakes across the sky in jagged formations. 'I know a place.' Josh yells above the rumbling thunder as we race back across campus. By the time we enter a house on Professor Row I don't have time to admire the architecture. Rain is pouring down in sheets. Biting my lip I know my shirt is soaked and transparent.

'Come through to my room and I'll get something you can change into.' Ugh. He's laughing at me. I know it.

CHAPTER NINE

Dinner with the Professor

With wet hair and rain streaming down between us I didn't think that Josh would recognise me but now my confidence was at an all-time zero. I had never been caught out incognito before and I hoped that Josh could be cool about it. What was left of my 'Millie' persona had been washed away with the temporary hair dye under the hot water of the shower.

Rolling up the cuffs of his pants and folding down the waistband a couple of times ensured that I wouldn't have an embarrassing wardrobe malfunction in the next few minutes. Tossing my wet hair up into a towel put off the inevitable questions for a few moments longer. His clothes were surprisingly comfortable. Putting on my big girl pants I exited the bathroom noticing that my wet clothes had already disappeared.

'It's still pouring out there. Won't be able to get back to your place tonight.' Josh entered the room with his hands tucked inside his front pockets to keep them warm, 'I put your things in the washing machine.' Arching an eye brow silently at him he quickly defended himself, 'I read the labels first.' All the unsaid words hung heavy in the air between us. They can wait. The boy looks like a drowned rat. His attempt to give me space is adorable. I can't tell him I grew up in a one-bathroom house with a brother who thought the mirror had been hung for his personal use.

'Okay.' I reply still shivering. There was no hairdryer in the bathroom and I'm trying to dry my hair with an already damp towel. 'Here.' He tosses me a grey hoodie from the stack of clean laundry on the end of the King size bed occupying a large corner of the room. Slipping it over my head it envelopes me in a huge hug.

'I grew.' He shrugs. 'I like oversized shirts.' I admit. He snags some clean clothes and shuts the door of the bathroom. Curling up in the corner of his overstuffed black two-seater couch I pick up the book off his side table. Studying the spine, I smile to myself. I understand the beauty of a thick book. He's reading George R. R. Martin- A Dance With Dragons.

Opening the book to the page he has marked I easily lose myself in the story. The sound of the bathroom door knob turning startles me out of the story after about twenty minutes. Closing the book carefully so I don't dislodge his folded piece of paper from between the pages, I lay the book back where I found it. He's leaning against the wall across the room observing me with a small smile. His usually carefully styled hair is still damp and messy.

'So, I guess you have some questions?' I ask holding up a lock of extremely obvious blond hair. 'The brunette was awesome but the blond suites you too.' he quips easily holding out his hand for the damp towel I've folded up and left on the floor in front of me. Disappearing for mere moments he joins me on the couch when he returns. I decide to tackle this head on. Holding out my hand to him I introduce myself, 'Pleased to meet you Joshua Patterson. My name is Lily la Croix.'

Taking my hand, he shakes it gently before enveloping it between both of his hands warming it further, 'So what do I call you now? Millie or Lily?' I take my time replying. I want to give Josh something real. Something concrete he can hold onto after I go back to the claustrophobia of another round of press interviews and the book tour. 'Neither.' I say surprising myself, 'My real name is Amelie. No one calls me that anymore. When we're alone can you call me Amelie?'

(Josh)

There's underlying pleading note in the tone of her voice. 'Amelie.' I murmur before really taking in the oversized clothes on her slight figure, her still drying blond locks and the way she's trying to conceal the fact that she's still shivering.

Pulling at the blanket I keep folded up along the back of the couch it drops down on top of her head. Soft giggles erupt from her mouth. Her whole face changes lighting up the room. Deftly tucking the blanket around her she stares up at me like a deer caught in the headlights of an oncoming car.

'Are you hungry?' I tuck an errant curl back behind her ear. 'I make a mean hot chocolate.' I add. She swallows. Colour stains her cheeks. 'Hot chocolate sounds good.' She replies her words measured as if she's still waiting for a big reaction to her superstar status. 'I'm not going to bring the press down on your head princess.' I promise her quietly, 'When you're ready to tell me everything you will.'

(Millie)

'Josh!' A male voice echoes from another part of the house. He freezes halfway across his room and face palms his forehead before giving me a rueful smile, 'I forgot. Sorry one uncomfortable family dinner coming up.'

He watches me put the pieces together in my head. Patterson. Professor Patterson also known as the Dean of students. Oh Crap! He nods sagely knowing I've made the connection. 'Who else?' I ask my voice starting to sound thready in desperation. 'Ryan.' Josh answers before scooping up a slouch beanie.

Watching me pluck it out of the air with satisfaction Josh adds, 'You should be able to conceal your hair…mostly.' His footsteps thump up the stairs to respond to the professor's call. Tucking my hair up into the beanie I leave some curls free before reaching for my bag. Retrieving my thick frames, purple leather bracelet and a nude lip stain gloss the adjustments to my new disguise is complete.

'What else do you have in your little bag?' Josh's voice startles me. He's leaning against the door jamb watching my movements with interest. 'Is it like the undetectable extension charm Hermione does in Harry Potter?' He asks. Unable to contain my laughter, I let it roll out echoing off the stone walls.

'Careful camera boy. Your geek side is peeking out.' I manage to say as I struggle to catch my breath. 'Inhaler?' He asks without missing a beat. Gesturing to my bag I focus on slowing my breathing down. I feel the inhaler being pressed into my hand. I hate asthma with a passion. Takes the fun out funny. Waiting for my breathing to return to normal I slip the inhaler into the front pocket of my hoodie.

'Your geek side is showing?' Ryan's voice is filled with amusement, 'If I knew you were having company I would have declined the invitation to dinner.' Josh squeezes my hand under the blanket before turning to face his friend, 'You can talk. You're a bigger Potterhead than I am.'

'I don't believe we've been introduced.' Ryan addresses me. I cut him off my voice filled with amusement, 'I watched your sister yell at you for a good 30 minutes today. Creative Writing for Dummies 101 ring a bell?' 'That was you?' He finally asks with a shrug. 'That was you?' Josh echoes before Gibbs slapping Ryan up the back of the head. 'Yeah.' He admits sheepishly, 'Cassie already embarrassed me about it. It was Millie, right?'

'Yep.' I pop the p breaking the uncomfortable atmosphere. 'I like you.' He declares, 'You call it like you see it. I like that.' Josh stands in front of me with his hands on his hips, 'Get in line. I call dibs.' Another voice interrupts the squabble threatening to break out in front of me, 'You can't call dibs son if you don't feed the girl first.'

Dinner is an interesting affair. Ryan and Josh act like blood brothers and the Professor treats them equally. The air is filled with laughter, love and a lot of pride. After dinner, the professor leads me to a guest bedroom. There's a child's crib and toys in a box stacked neatly against one wall. 'Ryan usually sleeps on the couch downstairs and I don't think it's appropriate for you to share Josh's bed under the circumstances Miss la Croix.' The Professor states calmly not inferring anything.

It's what he isn't saying that leaves me bristling with irritation. The media paints me as a starlet hopping from one actor to another sports star to a music artist on a weekly basis. Even worse the media likes to speculate who I may or may not be seeing at any given time. It's almost a crime to have male friends of any kind.

'I would have slept on the couch.' My cheeks are unbearably hot, 'Despite what the media says I'm not that kind of girl.' Wrapping the edges of my tattered dignity around myself I step backwards into the room before shutting the door in the Professor's face. Solid thumping sends vibrations through the door. Steeling myself against another parental admonition my hand turns the door handle slowly.

'I heard.' Josh's face is one of concern. I don't reply to his statement instead I open the door a little wider. 'For the record Amelie, ' he smiles down at me, 'I don't think you're that kind of girl either.' Before I can respond he kisses me. A brief touch of his lips against mine. Unbidden my fingers steal to my lips in wonder, 'I wasn't expecting that.' 'Wanted to give you something to look forward to.' he admits watching me gather my non-existent thoughts before asking, 'Need a shirt to sleep in?' Shaking my head, I smile at him as I close the door, 'Your hoodie will do fine.'

CHAPTER TEN

Drinks?

My eyes swept around the unfamiliar room landing on the neat pile of clothing on the chest of drawers just inside the door. Changing into my own clothes, I threw Josh's hoodie back on to guard against the chill in the air. Straightening the bed cover I left the room as neat as I found it. 'Not sneaking out, are we?' Josh's amused voice greets me the moment I stepped into the family room. Growing hot under his scrutiny my blush gives me away easily. 'Press.' I explain before striking a pose,

'Lily la Croix was seen exiting house of College Dean in the early hours of this morning. No comment yet from either party. Stay tuned for further developments on this new story in the recently reticent author's life. Would make everyone's lives hell for a few weeks until it was all straightened out.' 'Somebody needs her morning coffee.' Josh held out his mug as a peace offering.

Wrinkling my nose slightly at the bitter taste the professor made an appearance in a frilly apron, 'Press can't get to you here. Miss la Croix. I hope pancakes are alright.' Holding back the giggles that bubbled up from my stomach I made a face at Josh. He made a silly one back at me and the laughter spilled from my lips. 'Josh loves to give gag gifts.' the professor pouted at me waving the spatula like a laser pointer, 'You have been forewarned.' Forewarned was forearmed. Raising an eyebrow over the liquid energy I continued to sip I watched the banter continue between father and son. Who knew that after such a frosty reception that they would be a lot more relaxed.

After they snuck me back onto the campus proper I didn't hear from Josh. He stole my first kiss from me in such a sweet way. He didn't need to know I was a dating virgin. Was I supposed to brag that the infamous Josh Patterson had kissed me to the entire world via social media and that it was somewhat complicated? How would that have made me any different to the swarm of barbies that followed him from class to class?

Days passed. Snowed under with work I barely noticed until he called me early one morning. 'Morning Josh.' I greet him bouncing a little from my third cup of coffee.

'How much caffeine have you had this morning Amelie?' His laughter tinges his voice. 'One cup.' I try innocently. Maybe I could hide the fact that I now had my own coffee machine in the dorm.

'Plus?' He's not going to let this go and it occurs to me that we're totally having a Gilmore Girls moment here. He's not Luke and I'm no Lorelai.

'Plus two but in my defence, I was working on a really difficult passage of the book.' Popping a blue m & m into my mouth I let it melt while he talks.

'Want to go for drinks tonight before class?' His voice sounds a little gravelly. He sounds like he's getting a head cold. Taking my hesitation as a bad thing he rushes to reassure me, 'I know a place where we won't be hassled.'

'Ok.' I could do with a bit of freedom. All I ever do is work and I want to spend time with him again. 'Okay as in yes?' He sneezes. 'Bless you.' The words slip automatically out of my mouth before I ask, 'Should you be resting?'

'I'll be alright.' I hear snuffling in the background. He's blowing his nose.

'What's the name of the place? I'll meet you there. I have some meetings off campus today.' I eye my packed garment bag making a face at it. Days like these required multiple outfit changes to keep everyone happy.

'It's the Lakeside Village Tavern. I'll send coordinates to your phone. I thought you were restricted to campus.' He sounds genuinely confused.

'My publicist wants me to be seen and photographed today. My agent has set up a photo shoot for a magazine article and my parents are meeting me for lunch.' I sigh softly. In other words, once the paps get wind that I'm in town I won't be able to move more than a few meters without a camera being shoved in my face.

'Your security detail will be with you, right?' He asks all levity gone from his voice. 'Jenny will be beside me and Dave is driving.' I hasten to add for his benefit, 'She's my bodyguard and he's the additional muscle.' He doesn't say anything for a minute. That's when the proverbial penny drops. 'You're my unofficial bodyguard, aren't you?' I should be furious. 'I'm anything you need me to be Amelie.' His voice cracks slightly, 'Will you meet me tonight?'

'Only if you promise to do one thing for me.' Nick had a lot of explaining to do when I got hold of him. 'Anything.' One word accompanied by another sneeze. 'Take the day off from classes. I'll write you a note if you need one.' Moving to my freezer I withdraw a frozen container I have been saving for an emergency. I pop the container into the microwave and locate my thermos. 'Alright.' He agrees. 'What dorm are you in?' I ask switching to my ear piece so I can work hands-free.

'Green 205. Why?' he asks. I smile to myself as I reply, 'I'll be over in the next ten minutes.' Thank gosh for a mother who plans for every emergency. I had enough cold supplies to surplus an army. I throw everything into my tattered backpack.

Locating his dorm room is incredibly easy. He lives in a boys only building. I knock three times on his door and wait. Ryan answers with a smile, 'Millie. I wouldn't come any further if I were you. He's like a bear with a sore tooth this morning. Between you and me that's not a pretty sight.' 'Left or right?' I ask entering their shared space. Typical boys' room. Stacks of games line one wall along with a gigantic Tv. The game console and controllers are hastily shoved to one side as if I've disturbed him in the middle of his pursuit for the freedom of mankind or some such ignoble quest.

'Right.' He shrugs one shoulder, 'You were warned. Tapping on the door lightly I wait for his permission to enter. When I do he's lying across his queen bed wearing a Henley shirt and track pants. 'What are you doing here?' he asks as I open my backpack. 'I brought you supplies so you don't have to deal with the barbies. Everything you need to beat the flu. My mum's chicken soup, decongestants, cough lollies, tissues, chocolate and a limited-edition copy of The Day of the Doctor.' I feel awkward. This is outside of anything I've experienced before. 'I would have gotten you a movie with a hot chick but I didn't know which starlet you're crushing on.' I explain with a quick smile, 'Usually, anything with Channing Tatum works for me.' 'Channing huh?' He raises an eyebrow, 'Wonder what he'd say about that?'

'Actually, he was really sweet.' I perch carefully on the edge of his bed, 'Signed a copy of Magic Mike for me over a coffee. Would have been a Whiskey and Coke but I'm not allowed to drink on the job.' I check the time on his bedside clock. I'm going to be running closer to my appointment than I would have liked.

'I'd kiss the ever-loving daylights out of you but you have to go to work.' His hand finds mine on the bed, 'Are you sure you're not angry I hid stuff from you?' Meeting Josh's eyes, I reassure him, 'I was at first. You didn't have to talk to me or invite me out. You don't make me feel like

I'm just the client or someone famous who dropped her panties for you. You make me feel human.'

'Dropped her panties?' Of course, he'd focus on the one questionable phrase used in the whole monolog. I can feel my face blush in response. Taking pity on me he squeezes my hand, 'Be safe today.' 'Always.' I promise before leaving.

He doesn't pry. I like that about him. Opening the door to my Toyota Corolla Conquest pain shoots up both arms. Today was supposed to be a well-deserved break for pounding the keyboard until small blisters have appeared on my fingertips. Grimacing I reach for the wrist braces I had Nick conceal in the glove box. This was the other secret I kept from the world. Tendonitis.

It's just on seven pm when I pull into the parking lot at the Lakeside Village Tavern. I think I managed to give a quality interview. Slipping the wrist braces off I place them on the seat beside me. My stylist found a cute red dress last minute. Josh is waiting outside. I wait until he's finished his cigarette before getting out of the car.

Those things are going to kill him. His lungs his choice. I chose not to be around it. 'Hi.' I greet him with a smile. 'Hey writer girl.' A slow grin spreads across his face, 'Deny you dressed up for me. I dare you.' 'I dressed up a little.' I admit playing his game feeling his heavy jacket settle around my shoulders, 'Thanks. I didn't have time to run back to the dorm for a jacket.'

He leads me inside to a secluded table in the corner with a reserved sign on it. 'Whiskey and coke, right?' He asks after I'm settled. I nod. He makes his way through the Friday night crowd to the bar. A glass of ice is placed in front of me breaking me out of my favourite hobby of observing the people around me. Josh places an unopened can beside it then pulls a straw out of his pocket. He pulls another can from his back pocket with ease before sitting down opposite me.

'You look stunning.' He says quietly. 'Thanks.' I take a sip my drink. His phone plays a snippet of Skillet's Say Goodbye. 'Jed and Norah are here.' His eyes harden. Reaching across the table I squeeze his hand in sympathy, 'What do you need?' He drains half his can before replying, 'Nothing. Be ready to move if a fight breaks out.' Jed and Norah make their way through the restaurant side of the tavern towards us along with the waitress bringing us a garlic bread. She places it on the table with a flirty little smile aimed in Josh's direction.

He keeps his eyes on mine. Picking up a piece of the garlic bread he holds it to my lips. Feeding me. A deliberate gesture. For whose sake? Jed places his beer to my right and Norah takes the seat on my left. Tension rolls off her in waves. 'Jed.' Josh greets his brother.

(Josh)

Her brow creases slightly fingers tightening a little more in mine. The side of her lips quirk up at the sight of the karaoke equipment. Raising her eyebrow at me she asks, 'Ready for this?' 'What?' Leaning back in my seat I watch as she manoeuvres her way out of the Jed and Norah sandwich. 'This.' She winks at me before busting out the lyrics to Gold Digger. She's hamming it up on stage to make up for her obvious lack of talent. 'Girl can't sing for shit.' Norah comments sneaking some of our garlic bread. She follows it up with a decent rendition of You Don't Own Me before sitting down beside me on an obvious high.

'Got your number.' she bluntly levels at Norah, 'I think it's high time we had some girl talk to get the bile off your chest before it sours your face any further.' She drains her drink and beckons for Norah to follow her to another table. 'Girl's got guts.' Jed mutters to me as we strain to hear their conversation, 'My money's still on Norah. She fights dirty.'

(Millie)

'Did you really interrupt our date to fight with me or was there a bigger reason?'

I lead off with suddenly tired of the day's drama. Idiots had dogged my every footstep from the minute I had appeared for my first appearance. 'Jed is sick. Clarity is starting to pick up on it.   Josh needs to take her more than once a month.' She points a finger at me, 'That shit you pulled with the microphone was so not funny.' Jed's sick. Clarity?   A sick feeling in my stomach confirms the stray suspicions in my mind. 'Niece?' 'Daughter.' Norah's mouth stretches into a knowing smile, 'Haven't had the previous partners chat yet have you?'

'Would have but you crashed my date.' I pointed out reasonably and continued, 'So you need him to step up. What's your real problem with me then?' 'Don't want to be replaced by you.' she breathes a stray tear streaking a black line down her face. Handing her a napkin, I wait silently for her to continue, 'Clarity is pure sunshine on a cloudy day. I don't want her to forget me okay.' 'I wouldn't let that happen.' I try to reassure her. She sizes me up before lunging erratically at me, 'If you're playing me, I'll kill you!'

Over the top. Jed appears to pull the distraught woman into his chest. An arm drops around my shoulders. 'Do we need to separate you two?' Josh asks half seriously. 'Nope.' I reply pasting a slightly bored expression on my face, 'That's your definition of scary? Really? You'll have to do better than that if you want to make me cower in front of you. Not all deaths are the same Norah. Some of us have dignity.' Checking my watch, I'm startled to see how fast the time has flown.

'I have a class to teach in 30 minutes. See you after?' Josh's face drops slightly before he replies, 'I'll be there. Keep the jacket. It's cold outside princess. You can give it back to me tomorrow.' He walks me to my car.

(Josh)

She's waiting for me under the lights at the end of class. 'Want to come to mine for coffee?' She reads my mind and adds, 'I do mean coffee camera boy.' Too much has happened tonight. The sneezes I've managed to quell ring out in a series like gun shots. Sympathy flits across her pretty features. 'Another time?' another sneeze fills the air between us. 'Sure.' She agrees.

CHAPTER ELEVEN

Shared secrets

(Millie)

Josh's secrets lie heavy on my heart. He's been so tired lately I've hesitated to bring up what Norah told me with him. We've been two planets rotating in symphony around each other never stopping long enough to spend time together. Picking up my phone my fingers fly over the virtual keypad.

Can you spend a few hours with me today? I know a completely secluded place no one ever goes.

Pacing in front of the glass wall in front of me I stop long enough to rest one hand on the window. I'm getting cabin fever. I need out. Feeling the vibration in my other hand I glance at the screen long enough to read his message.

Sure. Lunch?

Short. Right. He had a visual arts class. I kept my reply equally as brief.

Bring it with you. I'll bring mine.

I must have piqued his imagination because another text arrived within seconds.

You're being super secretive writergirl. I'll need directions to your hideaway.

Follow the lane past the garden café. Hang a right at the lamp post. Meet me at the park bench.

No Lion, Witch or Wardrobe lol I'll c u at 12.30 :)

I send him the thumbs up emoji before tossing my phone on my neatly made bed. Checking the time, I hurry into the bathroom to get ready for the day. I had to survive a meeting with 'she who decided my life' first. Racing past the front desk with a quick wave of apology in their general direction I burst into the meeting room completely out of breath. Eyes narrowing at the scene in front of me I processed the immediate implications. Shit.

Julie shakes her head and points at the free seat at the head of the table forcing me to walk around the room. Judgement hangs heavy in the air. Sliding my iPad silently from my bag I open the app I need to take notes. That's when I notice I forgot to remove the braces. Oh goody. Cue the lectures. 'Right.' Julie punctuates the end of the last point before turning to address me, 'Lily how soon before you're done with rewrites?' 'Realistically?' Her eyes darken at the sight of my braces. Swallowing I continue, 'If there are no more photo shoots, press or meet and greets scheduled I could probably be done in two months.' Sue flips through my schedule, 'I don't have anything on the books except for a radio commitment in August.' 'Schedule some cortisone injections, time with a physio and use the damn speech to text program IT installed on your computer last time.' This last sentence is directed at me as if by being injured I've somehow committed some grave error showing my unprofessionalism.

She writes July on the board and circles the word almost daring me to cause a fuss. 'Can we discuss your book tour for a moment?' She carries on when no one says a word, 'Sue.' Sue smiles and takes the floor metaphorically, 'Right. We're going out big with a stop in the capital of every major country in the world. When you get to Singapore we'll leak it that you're in talks with Hollywood to have Lilac Cove turned into a movie series. From there we'll start a new campaign built on the hysteria from that.'

Nodding I pretend to play along with the horrific work schedule she's just spelt out to me. 'Realistically Sue. How long are we talking about? Eight weeks? Twelve weeks? Who are you planning to hook me with up this time round?' Normally I don't even question what she does. All chatter ceases instantly. 'I'm looking at least twelve weeks and we've been in talks with Uriah Shelton's management, Dylan Sprouse needs a leg up and Cole Sprouse's management hasn't gotten back to us yet.'

I'd definitely love to spend time with Uriah Shelton and Cole Sprouse but I don't know what kind of definition to put on what's happening with Josh. 'Can I get back to you on that?' I ask and word my next sentence very carefully, 'I might have a someone in my life. I don't want to jeopardize anything and no you do not have permission to leak that anywhere.' I give the whole table my best ice queen glare, 'This is one area in my life that is off limits understand?' 'I'll need to know as soon as possible.' Sue makes a note in her day planner keeping the atmosphere professional when it's obvious she wants to delve deeper behind my statement.

Clutching my takeaway container in one hand and my much-needed coffee in the other I arrive at my secret thinking spot five minutes late. Stretched out length ways on the bench hand tucked behind his head Josh was staring up at the sky deep in contemplation. 'Hi.' Blocking his view, it takes him a few minutes to come back to reality. Shaking it off he sits up abruptly, 'You look nice.' Making room for me beside him he grins sheepishly. 'I had a meeting with my team today. They're pushing for me to finish a month early amongst other things. 'Can you handle their demands?' he pulls a paper bag up off the ground from under the seat along with his own plastic go cup.

'I don't know.' I've never admitted defeat to anyone but Nick before. Taking a couple of mouthfuls of my sweet and sour pork I continue, 'They want me to be seen with a couple of unattached talent on the rise on the publicity tour.' He stills waiting for me to continue. 'I told them that I might have someone in my life who would object to the usual media stories.' My words meet dead air hunching forward I wrap both hands around my coffee. He's not making it any easier for me. 'How long is the publicity tour?' It sounds like he's weighing his words carefully as well. 'Twelve weeks.' I reply adding, 'A different city every day. More countries than I care to count.' His life will go on in the same pattern class, study, parties and spending time with his daughter. Mine will be crazy. 'What is this Josh? Can you define it for me?' I look up at him, 'I know there's a lot we skate over. What are you hiding from me?'

(Josh)

'I don't owe you anything.' The words fly out of my mouth before I have a chance to filter them. Her eyelids droop down shuttering her eyes. Hiding her true feelings from me. She wanted to know how I felt about her and I attacked her. Fuck! Her next words astonish me. 'You don't do you. I appeared out of nowhere and disrupted your life.' her voice is thick with tears, 'I'll be gone again soon enough and you won't have to worry about me on top of Jed's illness, your daughter and school.' Her words replay in my head '*Jed's illness, your daughter and school.*' Gathering her rubbish together, she's about to leave when I grab her wrist. She flinches and that's enough to have me pushing up the sleeves of her jacket so that I can see the thin black webbing of wrist braces.

'What?' I can barely get the words out of my mouth before she explains, 'Tendonitis.' A tear escapes from the corner of her eye and I let it keep rolling down her cheek unchecked. 'Amelie,' Even I can hear the pleading in my voice for her to stay, 'do they know what this is doing to you?' Nodding her head, she explains that the IT department at the publisher's set her up with a speech to text program a couple of years ago and that she's due to start therapy in a few days.

'How long do you have to wear the braces?' I want to pull her into my arms and cradle her gently protecting her from the world. I don't. Her body is stiff. Life isn't fair sometimes and even the shiny people have tiny flaws that get airbrushed over. 'Another week.' She answers once she's got her emotions under control. 'I can't talk about Clarity with you yet.' I open up to her giving her a hint of how much stress I've been under, 'I just got partial custody of her back and there's a lawyer involved.'

(Millie)

'I shouldn't have assumed that you would if I asked.' I offer tentatively. 'Norah doesn't know how sick Jed really is.' He blurts out, 'He wants to come back to stay with Dad.' No wonder he wants to reconnect with Josh. 'Is it…is it cancer?' my words fail me when he nods tightly. Sliding my arms around him I hug him as tightly as my wrists will let me. 'Fast moving and terminal.' he adds before asking, 'How many more books do you have left on your contract?' Resting his chin on top of my head I can feel him slowly relaxing again. 'This is the last one.'

Changes are going to be made if they want to keep me in their stable of bankable Authors.

We sit in silence for a while allowing the Zen state of the overgrown garden calm our tired and battered souls. 'About your tour,' He begins carefully before kissing the top of my head, 'Tell them I object strongly to the usual media stories. In fact, I object to you hanging out with any guy hotter than me. Channing Tatum is off limits, Amelie.' 'Of course, he is.' My small smile widens slightly, 'He's married.' 'Separated.' he informs me, 'Happened in May if you can believe the magazines that Cassie leaves at our place.' 'So,' I ask him again softly, 'what are we?' 'We,' he kisses my forehead, 'are complicated, crazy and completely us.' He answers finally holding me close.

CHAPTER TWELVE

Stalker

With all the responsibilities piling up on Josh we stole the few hours over lunch to be together daily. He needed space to breathe and I needed time away from the keyboard. My phone began to play Heart is a Weapon by Walk off the Earth. I let it ring out until it reached the lyrics

> *'Your heart is a weapon*
>
> *Can't take it anymore*
>
> *Change your direction*
>
> *Stop banging on my door'*

Stabbing at the phone I slipped into my best bitch persona, 'Hello.' My frosty tones alerted Josh that this was no ordinary call. Slipping in my earpiece, I scrolled through my phone looking for my voice recording app hoping to keep the caller distracted with banalities. Josh's jaw clenched at the underlying threat in the easy-going tone loud enough for the world to hear.

'Underestimate me. That'll be fun.'

'For who Oliver, ' I loathed this guy deliberately keeping my tone syrupy sweet as I attempted to play him like a fiddle, 'you or me?' Exasperation swept over me at Josh's frantic hand signals. 'Oliver Green?' he mouthed the name at me before reading the disgust pouring off me in waves. 'Me of course.' his oily tone slithered through the line, 'I will find you doll. The world wants to see their precious darling Author's sordid secrets.' He always kept his insane promises too. He had questionable practices and even more questionable morals. The man was the best in the business at sniffing out celebs who dropped out of sight and refused to allow anyone to get in the way of his money shot.

'Now really isn't the best time for you to be playing games with my life. I need a break until this book is finished. I promise you can have an exclusive photo opportunity once I'm done.' I hoped by dangling a carrot to him he would take the bait. 'No can do. Even a blurry shot of you is worth money in my pocket. Got bills of my own to pay.' Oliver Green was officially hunting my ass. Great. Honesty meets harsh reality. Break time was over. Grimacing I listened to the spew of insinuations linking me with everyone from Oliver Cromwell to Johnny Depp.

Josh's eyes had turned icy and I needed to end the call before he opened his mouth. 'It's been interesting as always Ollie.' He hated being called Ollie. Swiping to end the call I felt frustrated with the complexities of my life. Emailing the recording of the voice call to Nick I waited for confirmation that he had received it. I knew the drill inside out and backwards. Time to destroy the chip. Turning the phone over in my hands I used a bobby pin to slide the chip tray out of my iPhone. Josh did the honours for me grinding it beneath the heel of his boot into small pieces without a word giving me the few precious minutes I needed to pull myself back together.

'The Oliver Green?' Josh found his voice. I could detect awe overlaid with a slow burning fury. 'The Oliver Green was trying to keep me talking so he could track the signal.' I took a yoga breath in and out struggling to maintain my calm, 'He's probably the worst vulture of them all.' I stared ruefully at the scattered pieces of the chip, 'I'll have to use a burner phone until someone can get a replacement for me.' 'I'll sort one out for you.' Determination infused his tone as he added, 'Until then I have a spare you can use. No one will connect a paper trail to Lily la Croix.'

Afterwards, things got weird. Little details out of place. Little things. It bugged me. I knew I was being watched. I would come home to find my clothes cupboard panels cracked open like I'd forgotten to shut them completely. My perfume bottle moved over half an inch on the bathroom vanity. Extra dishes I hadn't used in the dishwasher and my towel damp when I hadn't showered. I was well past creeped out. Emmie was embracing her inner Lily la Croix. I was clinging to my Millie persona in an attempt to keep flying under the radar. Oliver Green had rattled my cage and I was looking for monsters in all the shadows surrounding me. The problem was Emmie was changing just slowly enough for no one else to notice but me.

Ryan answered the door when I turned up at Josh's with a couple of overnight bags. 'At the sleepover stage, are we?' he commented before taking in my appearance fully. Bruises under my eyes from lack of sleep the most prevalent give away that something was really wrong. 'Come in.' His easy-going manner dissipating in an instant replaced by a wariness I'd only experienced from my security team.

He placed a cup of tea in front of me. 'Drink that. It'll help.' he informed me gruffly before adding, 'After it you're going to tell me why you're so terrified.' He hovered over me until I drained the cup. 'I know you live in the palace. Admin only put certain people in that suite. So how big of a name are you really?' He didn't mince his words. 'It won't go anywhere?' I needed to know that I could trust him. 'Josh would kill me if it did.' He admitted. Playing with the handle of the empty mug in front of me I released a breath before speaking, 'Lily la Croix.'

'And I called your course creative writing for dummies 101.' He laughed breaking the tension that had begun to fill the room. 'It was kind of insulting.' I pointed out with a small smile. 'I can imagine. Why are you terrified Lily?' He was like a dog with a bone. My smile faltered and then slipped away completely, 'My security has been compromised. At first, I thought I wasn't closing doors and putting things back in their spots. It's kind of hard to ignore the wet towels and extra dishes.' 'I'll need to review your security system and look at the latest recording.' He announced thinking it over before asking, 'How long Lily?'

'Two weeks.' I breathed out in frustration, 'The first thing I did was check that the system was working. Whoever they are they're good. Pre-recorded time loops to cover real time recordings. I left tiny slivers of paper in my doors only to find them on the floor. My place has been broken into numerous times in the past few days. There's this as well.'

Passing over my burner phone I pull up the recording of a figure creeping around the bed while I lay asleep. 'I hid a camera the moment I figured it out.' 'You need sleep.' He pronounced catching my yawn, 'We can pick this back up later. Have you let your security team know something's wrong?' 'Sent them everything I have this morning.' Picking up my bags he pushes me through Josh's door, 'He has classes for another four or five hours. Enough time for you to get some uninterrupted sleep. I promise you he will be furious about this. Make yourself at home. I have training to get to.'

Shouting invades my sleep. Fighting through the layers of fogginess I pick up on the fury and deep concern. 'She's in your room. I made her get some sleep...Lily did we wake you?' Ryan notices my presence before Josh does, 'I'm going to go scout through your place now. Is there anything else you want me to grab?' I can feel Josh's silent challenge. 'What?' he exclaimed running a hand through his hair, 'You didn't think that I was planning to skate by in life on a football scholarship and no fall-back plan. Damn man.' Hoping to diffuse the fight slightly I ask softly, 'Security?' 'Private security.' He confirms and elaborates, 'Bodyguard work specifically.' 'I brought anything I wanted with me.' I sneak a glance up at Josh's silent profile, 'Thanks Ryan.'

'Why didn't you come to me sooner?' Josh asks after the door closes behind Ryan. His eyes rake over my dishevelled appearance. 'Jed. Clarity. School.' I list my reasons off on my fingers, 'I ran when I saw the footage of the intruder in the same room with me sleeping.' Rubbing my shaking hands up my arms I look him dead in the eye, 'Anything could have happened. I know that okay. If I tell Nick this happened, he'll have me out of here so fast your head will be spinning. I wanted one more night here with you.' 'Amelie,' his hands enclose mine stilling their erratic movement, 'you can trust me not to fold under pressure. No matter what I have going on your important. I will come if you call me.'

He still looked angry. 'Is it Jed?' I asked softly as he pulled me into his arms. He had moved back in with the professor not long after the phone call from Oliver. 'He's changed.' He tightened his arms around me, 'I don't know how to act around him now. Too much time has passed. He's so sick every morning Amelie.' I held him back with every ounce of strength I possessed. Helplessness often went hand in hand with hopelessness. I didn't want Josh going there emotionally. 'And Clarity?' I couldn't help but ask after the little girl I hadn't met yet.

'Clarity doesn't understand much only that her 'daddy' can't play with her anymore and her other daddy doesn't want her to stay at Grandma's for too long.' He dropped his chin on top of my head, 'Can we just pretend that none of this exists tonight? Go choose a movie from one of the piles and I'll sort out some food.'

CHAPTER THIRTEEN

Point of Clarity

Just like that my time at the college was done. Lily la Croix had not resurfaced in the world yet and Millie no last name was almost no longer needed. I was back home where it was safe. Where the world could not intrude upon me at will. Where I often got lonely and craved interacting with people my own age. I missed the freedom of going out for coffee and wandering through a crowd unnoticed. My only point of normalcy was Josh's texts and phone calls. Right on cue my phone rings.

'I need a favour.' Josh's voice sounds slightly panicked. My gaze sweeps around my messy office desk. Papers are strewn across my table as I attempt to keep the continuity straight in my manuscript. 'I need you to watch my daughter for a few hours.' He continues without hesitation, 'I have some major scheduling conflicts today. Dad has classes. I have some tests today otherwise I'd blow off the lectures and Norah's just dropped Clarity off without any warning.' 'How long can you give me to get there?' I ask moving towards my bedroom for a quick change to hide my real persona.

'Forty minutes.' He replies. 'And if you forego the crowd of barbies between the cafe and class?' I ask quickly shoving my hair in a messy bun and placing a beanie over it. 'An hour.' I keep moving grabbing my glasses frames and large tote bag, 'All you have to do is entertain her at home for a while and then take her to the playground when she wakes up from her nap. Jed's got appointments at the hospital this morning so it will just be you and her until about 2 pm this afternoon.'

Pulling up in front of the professor's house I barely have a chance to exit the car before Josh is shoving Clarity into my arms. 'Thank you.' He kisses me quickly, 'Everything's inside and her car seat is by the front door.' 'Hi Clarity. I'm Millie.' Josh grins at us before bolting across the grass toward at breakneck speed. Clarity was a dream to watch after. We watched the kids channel until I deemed it time for snacks and then she went down for her nap with a bottle of lukewarm milk. I remembered warm milk helped me sleep when I was younger and thought that maybe she'd like that as well.

Cleaning up the mess we had made of the living area. I used the extra time to construct a blanket fort in the dining room using the table as a cavern and all of the chairs as anchors. Inside it I placed Clarity's books and a few surprise snacks as well as some cushions off the sofa.

We'd been at the park for 15 minutes when my phone rang. I had been pushing Clarity in the baby swing and kept the motion up single handed. 'I see you managed to crack another phone number Oliver.' My patience had run out. It was one thing to stalk me via phone but another completely to invade my living space while I was sleeping. I didn't feel comfortable out in the open especially with Clarity in tow. 'It all started with you sweetheart.' He replies in easy going tones.

'It did, didn't it. This whole stalkership started because I dared to write a book series that became insanely popular. Because on top of being successful I also happened to be pretty enough to attract your camera. Did you ever stop to think that just maybe by feeding the beast you also cross too many lines? Oh, I know you stop mere inches away from the legalities of intrusion but you bulldoze your way through ruining lives because you don't recognize the moral implications of invading lives. You keep just feeding the beast and making paper.

Out of what? My supposed life. Guess what Ollie everything about the life you see is carefully staged. Behind us are a legion of publicists and stylists who turn out the perfect little darlings that the public expect. You don't know the real me. You will never know the real me.'

      'So, tell me about the adorable child you're pushing on a swing then. Is she your secret love child? Oh Lily,' he purrs, 'I do so love it when you play hard to get.' Hanging up on him. I scan the area immediately spotting his trademark beanie and lip piercing. Shielding my action from sight I slip the chip out of my phone and drop it into the cup of coffee I had placed beside the nappy bag on the ground. Mentally thanking Ryan for insisting on a dual sim phone I switched across to the second one before lifting Clarity out of the swing. 'Come on sweetie we can't stay here all afternoon. Daddy will be home soon.' Gathering up our belongings I make sure to drop the coffee cup in the nearest bin.

We're in danger. I'm heading back to professor's place now. Lily

Making sure Ryan and Josh's numbers are both tagged I hit send. Driving erratically, I manage to evade both Oliver and the police. Nowhere is safe for Clarity as long as I'm with her. Thinking fast, I place her in the blanket fort and settle her down for a nap before leaving the room. My phone rings again. 'Nice try Lily but we both know I'm a master at this. Does your baby daddy live here?' Not deigning to reply to his crap I send the boys another text.

He knows I'm here. Clarity's safe. Hurry. L.

Don't leave. I'm across campus. Josh

Second that. I'm at training. We'll be with you soon. Ryan

They didn't want me to leave. A floorboard on the back porch squeaked. The kitchen doorknob rattled as someone tested it. Sliding down the wall I weighed up my options as he tested all the windows around the house. Slipping out the back door I pulled it shut and silently tested it. Deliberately stepping on the squeaky floorboard, I waited for Oliver to round the corner of the house before running towards campus. There had to be somewhere I could go that was safe.

(Josh)

Amelie's car was parked diagonally across the driveway. She had locked all the doors but left her handbag behind. Ryan slipped around the back making sure the intruder had left before coming through the back door slamming it loudly. Together we approached the blanket fort. Clarity lay in the centre surrounded by toys and snacks. Blinking up at us she whimpered. A warning cry of the oncoming screams that were about to follow if I didn't pick her up immediately.

Sliding her out of her hidey hole I rocked her silently. Ryan returned from his inspection of the rest of the house. In his hand was a mobile phone. On the screen was an unsent text message.

He's not going to leave us alone. I will meet you at the Garden Cafe at 4 pm. If I don't show up, go to Nick. A. xx.

Ryan went to meet her. Four pm came and went without any sight of Amelie. Twirling the business card Nick gave me in my fingers I dialled the number without hesitation. 'It's Josh Patterson. She's in trouble.'

CHAPTER FOURTEEN

If this is a game I'm not playing

'Suspects?' Nick's all business now. I wonder what he does for a living.

'Oliver Green.' The guy's a scumbag. I can't believe that I idolised him once.

'Give me your number. That way you're not continually contaminating the crime scene.' He takes my digits and then says, 'Between us, we will get her back. Start thinking. Any detail could help.' 'Check into Norah. She only goes by the one name like Beyoncé. She works at the club over on eleventh. She threatened Amelie's life when she found out I was into her.' Might as well kill two birds with one stone, 'Also Ginny Patterson. The owner. My mother. She's got some kind of agenda that includes me dropping out of school and giving up custody of my daughter.'

'I'll call you back tonight. Keep thinking. You've already given the police three solid leads. They're going to want to talk to you and all her friends.'

'Nick.' I stop him mid flow of words, 'she works harder than anyone I know. I can count her acquaintances and friends on one hand. When we find her promise me things are going to change. 'I can't promise anything other than we will find her.' He's good at reassuring people.

He's one of those men who oozes with confidence. Nick meets me at the police station. 'I'll be with you in the interview as your lawyer.' He waits for me to finish my cigarette. Nerves kicking in.

I've got nothing to hide. I know the deal. Boyfriends are always the first person they examine as a suspect.

'Any history with the police?' he asks casually. Oh, he's good. I nod grinding the butt of the cigarette out with the toe of my boot. 'Juvenile stuff. Warnings mostly. Illegal car racing. Brawling. Gambling.' He nods tightly absorbing what I have to say. I can see the gears of his brain change up with the new knowledge. 'Jed Patterson is my brother.' I add knowing that they will bring it up inside.

Ryan joins us on the pavement. 'Ryan Western.' He introduces himself. 'You were the one who got her to call her security team.' Nick says as he shakes his hand. 'Yeah.' He's upset with himself. Has been since we figured it out. 'Also, the idiot who told her to use herself as bait.' He admits and adds, 'Cassie's been held up but she'll be here as soon as class lets out.'

The interviews are brutal. No one is concerned with Cassie's feelings and she sits sobbing in Ryan's arms while we are waiting for permission to leave. Nick is constantly fielding phone calls from Lily's management team. Her security team turns up for their interviews and they look right through us like we don't exist.

Words. In the end they offer us empty platitudes. 'Why haven't your parents shown up?' Ryan asks what we've all been thinking. If it were me missing, Dad would be in here screaming at them to do their jobs instead of drinking coffee and pointing fingers. Nick's eyes harden and a muscle in his jawline tenses. 'They gave up being there for her when they co-signed her contract. If anything needs to get done she calls me in. At least I'll fight on her behalf. The ongoing income keeps them silent. I'd give anything just to have her back even if she never writes another word again.' He turns to me, 'Got a cigarette? It's going to be a long night.'

(Millie)

Hindsight is such a beautiful thing. It allows you to take out a memory, examine it at your leisure to dissect from all angles to understand what has happened. I didn't have the luxury of hindsight to work out where everything had gone so horribly wrong. I had been fighting through the layers of oppression that were holding me in the dark.

'She's coming to.' I knew that voice. From where? Why don't I remember going to bed? Why can't I move? My eyelids flutter open. I'm not in the last place I remember being. Two people move into my line of sight. Shit just got real. I can't believe what I'm seeing. Emmie and Oliver together. I'm so angry that I want to scream. 'Lily la Croix.' She purrs, 'so nice to meet the real you.'

The real me. I don't even know who I'm supposed to be anymore. Slipping into the ice queen persona is as easy as putting on a hoodie. People like her are beneath me. They only want to be friends for the notoriety of it. She will never understand how much I hate that part of my life.

'Emerson Rose.' No more comfortable Emmie. She's one of them now. 'It was so easy. You didn't even suspect me. You were too busy looking over your shoulder for Ollie.' Standing side by side I can see the strong family resemblance. Brother? Cousin? Father? I don't ask the questions bouncing around inside my head. It hurts too much to try to think straight.

She continues talking at a fast pace. We've moved from straight from 'surprise guess who' to 'super villain monologue' I want to tune her out but she gets right up in my face spitting the sentences out at me rapid fire, 'Your security camera system. Your laptop camera. Your tunnel system. Your private luxury dorm suite. Your belongings. How do you think your family will respond? Will it be your money or your life? Who will miss you? Josh won't. I'll make sure of it. Once I pay for the treatments his brother needs he'll forget all about you.'

I don't know this deranged woman in front of me. I always thought she was kind of angry but I thought it was part of her edgy charm. She's also showing how dense she really is. Josh doesn't want me to pay for Jed's treatments because it's too late for that option now. 'Emmie.' One word is all it takes for Oliver to call her off. He raises a camera and takes a photo using the flash without warning. 'I told you this would be fun Lily. Loosen up a little. You're going to be here for a while.'

Here. From what I can see of 'here' there isn't that much to it. A closet size room with no windows and a bare light bulb. The walls are so new that it hasn't been painted. The door has a grill cut into it so that privacy will be an issue. I don't have to worry about breathing. 'Why?' I force the word out knowing that I might not get an answer for their insanity. He crouches down beside me careful not to touch any part me, 'Because you're famous. Drama is good for business.' 'You've heard the phrase fake it until you make it? You know what Oliver? I've already made enough money in my career never to lift a finger ever again and I'm still faking it every day of my life.' I aim the next words at Emerson, 'Fame isn't everything. I wouldn't wish the way I've been forced to live on anyone. I would give anything to be able to write books and be a nobody at the same time. The world doesn't work that way. I have the spotlight for now but wait until someone tweets something, writes something, does something much more amazing I'll be yesterday's news.' Refusing to speak to my captors further I ignore them completely by shutting my eyes.

CHAPTER FIFTEEN

Gone girl

(Josh)

Dad and I sit on one side of the court room. My mother sits on the other. Norah is beamed in on a screen on the wall dressed in the latest in prison fashion. 'I have read through this file very thoroughly. The child in question Clarity Patterson is not in attendance is that correct? Why is she not here?' The judge addresses us all over the top of her glasses. Taking a deep breath, I rise to my feet, 'She is at home with my brother your honour. We believed that

making memories between them was
extremely important and will abide by
whatever decision the court deems
appropriate.' 'Under the circumstances, I'll
let it slide. It is customary for the child in
question to be at the hearing Mr Patterson.'
She gestures for me to take my seat before
addressing Norah.

'I see that you are in no position to
care for Clarity at the moment Ms
Whittaker. Care to explain why I should
even entertain the solution your lawyer has
provided me with?' We all wait to hear what
Norah has to say for herself. She doesn't
muck around for once and speaks honestly,
'Because I have been caring solely for
Clarity since her birth with the help of my
boyfriend and his mother. I have a solid job
and a roof over my head.' 'Yes.' the judge's
voice is clipped, 'I see that you do have
those elements in place. You do not have
however an excuse for the quantities of
drugs that were found in your apartment.
Despite attempting to provide adequate care

for Clarity you have also denied Mr Patterson access to his daughter.'

'I chose to let her believe that Jed is her father. She didn't know Josh.' Norah's pathetic excuse fools nobody as she attempts not to fidget under the judge's heavy gaze before she turns back to me, 'I have also read through the report documenting your situation Mr Patterson. While you are still studying, you also have adequate accommodation, child care and a steady income in place. Do you believe that you can continue to care for Clarity full time and continue your education?' 'Yes, your honour. I've spoken to administration about cutting from a full course load to carrying a part course load. It will take me longer to graduate but it will enable me to be a better parent. Clarity deserves at least one parent who will take her to bear picnics in the park and will be there for her before and after school. She deserves to know a home full of love and security. I want to provide that for her.'

'Your girlfriend is too famous for Clarity to ever be safe with you.' My mother spits furious that she was dragged into the police station for questioning. 'Ah yes. Your girlfriend is Lily la Croix. How do you intend to keep Clarity safe after Miss la Croix is found?' The judge's face shows her sympathy even though she keeps her voice impartial. 'My friend Ryan is almost a fully-fledged body guard. Once he has completed his training we intend to hire his services initially for Lily and to extend further to Clarity once she starts to attend school. Lily lives in a gated community. She has expressed an interest in having Clarity and I move in with her as our relationship progresses.' I have thought this out thoroughly. Dad pats my shoulder as we are released for a short recess to allow the Judge to deliberate over things further.

Dad answers his phone and his smile widens. Five minutes to go before I find out whether I can keep my daughter. Five minutes is all it takes for my Mother to realise that she has to actually talk to me nicely if she is to see Clarity again. 'Josh.' Dad gains my attention, 'They've found her. They know where Lily is and they're getting her now.' 'How? Where?' My own phone rings. 'Ryan.' I answer after checking the name on the screen. 'They've got her Josh. Lily's safe.' He adds, 'I'm out front.'

(Millie)

I'm tired. Filthy. Covered in my own excrement. Hungry. Thirsty. The list is ongoing and I have counted every nail in my holding cell more times than I care to remember. I refuse to break. I don't know how much more of Emerson's craziness I can handle. Yesterday she came in brandishing a pair of scissors and a box of hair dye. I don't even know what I look like anymore and the crazy thing is I don't really care. Maybe I got my wish after all and can slip back into anonymity after this whole ordeal is over. Oliver refused to talk to me after she gave me a makeover. All noise has ceased outside this cell. Outside the loudness of my own breathing. I count my breaths just to reassure myself I'm still alive.

Scratching another mark in the chipboard floor with my bobby pin I count the marks. Chills sweep through my body. I've already been here for four days. In another three I could be dead.

Exhausted by my own small movements I curl in around myself and close my eyes. Random thoughts dance through my mind in fragments. I dream of strange noises shaking the house. Voices. Screaming. A child with curly hair. The door of my cell being ripped off its hinges. I'm not sure what's real and what's not at this point, hoping for a miracle I open my eyes when I feel someone touch fingers lightly against a pulse point. The violent sounds of vomiting reach my ears from outside the door and I wince reflexively. My stomach tightens even more painfully. 'Is this her?' gentle hands examine me for identifying marks. 'Does it matter?' Another hand squeezes my hand in reassurance, 'We're going to get you out of here.' I have to try. 'Police?' I'm so weak but I need to know.

'Yeah honey.' The hand squeezes gently, 'Police. Stay with me now. We got you.' Fighting to keep my eyes open I feel them wrap me in a clean blanket like some victim you see on SVU. Shielding my face from the multiple mobile phones they wheel me towards the waiting ambulance. It's night time. The stars twinkle down at me greeting me in their own special way. I search the gathering crowd. There's only one face I want to see and he isn't here. White noise. All of it. I cooperate with the medics working on me. Questions threaten to spill out. How did they find me? What happened to Emmie?

Wait why do I even care? If she hadn't been so creepy I wouldn't be in a hospital on a drip right now. I wait two days gathering my strength. Talking to the police. My family. The key people on my team. Flowers arrive by the truckload. Too many to keep. 'This one's from a Josh Patterson.' Sue looks at me. She's volunteered to help me craft an appropriate reply to my fans from my hospital room. 'What does it say?'

I need to know. 'You owe me a proper date. Call me.' She looks up, 'Is this…' 'My boyfriend.' I finish for her and add, 'Could you please dial a number for me?'

Holding it to my ear I listen to the dial tone. One ring. Two. 'Amelie?' His voice. I missed hearing his voice. Tears roll down my cheeks relentlessly. 'Amelie?' His voice is a little more insistent now. 'Josh.' I fight to get past the lump in my throat. His words break through my fugue state. 'I'm right here baby. It's going to be ok.' 'I got your flowers.' I pause struggling with my breathing a little, 'I'm going to sound completely clingy but I need you. Can you come? Now? Tomorrow?'

'I'm here. Been parked outside the hospital ever since Ryan told me where you were taken.' He listens to my laboured breathing. Sue takes over the conversation. She opens the door and speaks briefly to the security guarding my room. 'This never happened.' she tells me gathering her belongings, 'If I were you I'd have him dial everyone and pitch a fit at them until they cave.'

He looks like he hasn't slept for a week. Ryan stares down my private security before they let Josh through. 'I'm going to take a seat right over there. If either one of them goes missing I'm going to walk right over you to find their asses.'

'He's pissed.' Josh greets me warily. All the tubes must look confusing to him. 'It's more than dehydration.' He states bluntly crossing his arms. 'They didn't feed me. Didn't hydrate me. Didn't walk me.' I stop. He taps his toe on the floor. 'Didn't let me near a toilet.' My voice wobbles as I continue, 'Took compromising photos of me. Threatened to sell me.' My voice cracks completely on the last two sentences and I fall silent before one more thought crosses my mind, 'Clarity? Is she alright? I couldn't let him near her.'

'Never took you for the goth type princess.' My hair. I've been avoiding the mirror in the bathroom. Instead of my own blond tresses she's given me ink black hair that somehow accentuate the unnatural paleness of my skin. 'Clarity's fine. I won custody. If anybody asks we're planning on moving in together in about six months' time.' He pulls a box out from under his jacket. A burner phone. He tosses it on the bed beside me before taking a seat in the only chair near my pillow. 'Turn this on and keep it on Millie. Keep it charged. I'm speed dial 1 and Ryan is speed dial 2.' He pulls an accessory out of his pocket and I realise it's a watch. 'I'm surprised your security team didn't already have you wearing one of these. Even when you're out of range of your phone it has an inbuilt emergency function.' He places it beside the bed. 'Josh.' He stops. I see what Ryan sees. His fear. His anger. His insecurity. 'Hey.' I say softly. 'Hey.' He smiles back at me. I know we're going to be alright.

I watch him fall asleep in the chair comfortable in the knowledge that I am loved. His fingers dance around mine in his sleep desperate to keep hold of me. It's early when Ryan enters the room the next day. 'I brought him a change of clothes.' He drops a bag at the end of the bed. 'According to your men in black, you will be receiving a visit from your parents at nine. Might not be a good idea to still be here before officially meeting them.' He directs the last sentence towards Josh who places a gentle kiss against the backs of my fingers.

All too soon Josh has finished using my private bathroom. Ryan has been reading the board above my bed. 'She's scheduled to move to another room this evening.' He points out. My anxiety levels rise at the thought of not seeing Josh again sending all the monitors into overdrive. 'Way to go idiot.' Josh Gibbs slaps Ryan up the back of the head.

Turning back to me he presses his lips against my forehead. 'I'll find you.' He promises gently. I think of something else, 'You might want to come in the back door. They know who you are now.' 'Amelie.' His voice makes me feel safe. 'Yes Josh?' 'Get some rest princess.' He stops and turns around, 'And don't forget to keep your phone turned on.' Josh reminds me before placing it in my hand, 'I'm on one. Ryan's on two.' He kisses me again before Ryan physically drags him out of the door.

CHAPTER SIXTEEN

Meet my boyfriend

My parents. The last time I had spoken to my mother I had literally begged them for help and they had reminded me I needed to pay their salary. Nick arrived first. His eyes raked over me reassuring himself that I was still in the hospital bed he had left me in. 'They're on the way.' He informed me and added, 'If you need another day I can get the doctor to stall them again.' I shook my head gingerly, 'It's time Nick. I can't hide out here forever.' He took the seat closest to my head. 'Not that one. It's reserved.' He moves and watches me place my laptop on the seat. 'Anyone I know?' he continued in the same teasing manner, 'Tall, blue eyes, double major with a camera permanently slung over his shoulder maybe?'

'Definitely.' I can hear a three-ring circus approaching my room. My father's voice is booming as he demands the staff meets his expectations. My mother's heels disturb what little peace is left. The nurses are desperately trying to shush them and from somewhere I can distinguish the hurried gate of my doctor rushing to head them off. 'Family only.' He snaps at the media before indicating to security to escort them off the premises yet again.

Nick straightens in his seat automatically angling his body so they have to greet him first. 'Nicholas.' My Father enters the room followed by the socialite I am forced to call Mother. He scans the board above my bed before meeting my eyes. 'Lily.' I can feel his disappointment emanating off his body in waves. 'Lily what have you done to your hair?' Nick intervenes immediately, 'Remember I told you about this Mother. Find something appropriate to say or don't say anything at all those are the rules while your here.' 'When are you allowed home?' she ventured again a little more timidly.

'Next week.' my voice still sounds scratchy to my ears. 'What's this we hear about you dating a boy with a daughter in tow?' my father asks getting straight down to business. 'The boy has a name, ' I begin to stand up for myself. Nick stops me with a shake of his head. In the doorway is the largest bouquet of flowers I've seen in my life. 'I'll take that sir.' my personal nurse pops out of nowhere with a cheerful smile. Josh appears from behind the flowers. His first reaction is the same as the one Nick had. Check to see that I'm right where he left me. 'Hello Princess.' He greets me with a smile and does some weird bro handshake thing with Nick. Raising both my eyebrows I really didn't think that I'd been away that long.

'I checked with the doctor before I came to see whether we could extend the family rule for a few minutes.' He half turns to someone just out of sight. 'Mellie.' Clarity sits in his arms wearing a fancy pink dress. 'Careful now.' Josh warns her as he manoeuvres her close to my face, 'Mellie has plenty of boo boos.' Her milky breath assaults my senses before she plants a wet kiss on my cheek, 'Clarry kiss your owies all better.' she announced daring the adults in the room to contradict her. Pressing my lips against her forehead I whisper my thanks to her before Josh announces that Uncle Ryan knows where the fountain of chocolate milk is hidden. He leaves the silent room momentarily. 'Joshua Patterson and his daughter Clarity.' I inform my parents quietly, 'The child I was babysitting when everything happened.'

Mum and Dad exchange concerned glances. 'I'm going to keep seeing Josh.' I inform them bluntly. Nick squeezes my hand before speaking up in our defence, 'I've checked into him. Spent time with him. If he hadn't called me that she was missing, we may have never found Lily until it was too late. Something else you need to consider, Amelie's nineteen and technically she doesn't need your permission to have a normal life.' 'While we're on the subject of age, 'I speak up again, 'The next contract will not include any parent guardian clauses. The pay checks are going to stop. Realistically they should have stopped at eighteen. Things are going to change. Nick will take your questions about all this at a later date.' He nods in affirmation, 'Now's not the time to be thinking about business sister mine.'

'Sister mine?' Josh's low voice bounces off the walls in his astonishment, 'You basically labelled her yours and put a neon light over her for effect.' 'He did, didn't he.' I laugh and then wince frowning. 'No more making the pretty lady laugh then.' he kisses my forehead and settles back in his chair examining my parents with undisguised interest, 'Josh Patterson.' My machines hum steadily and beep three times before my father introduces them, 'George and Elizabeth St. James. You have a beautiful daughter.' Josh's face cracks into a smile.

'That's her public persona. Should have seen the fight I had to go through to get her into the dress.' He chuckles. 'That bad?' I ask to fill the silence, 'How's Jed?' His face drops slightly. 'He's hanging in there. Says he needs you to come read to him sometime soon.' The words are pulled from him. 'I thought you only had a daughter.' My father is confused. 'Jed is Josh's brother. He isn't doing so well right now.' Nick informs them before looking at his watch, 'Come on. Our time's up and the press is waiting for your statement.' 'Nothing too awful please.' I beg, 'Stick to the story they already have. Dehydration. Fragility and all that.'

Nick rushes them out before they can say anything insensitive. His eyes meet mine above Josh's head. I can expect him to return soon. 'Don't sugar coat it because I'm lying in a hospital bed. How is Jed really doing?' My voice cracks slightly startling me. I feel guilty. He needs to be at home with his brother not here with me. 'He's stable at the moment.' He brushes my fringe back from my eyes, 'Don't fret. I'm right where I need to be.'

CHAPTER SEVENTEEN

This is us

'This right here.' He whispers in my ear, 'This is us.' Craning my head around to meet the hidden laughter in his eyes I allow a lazy smile to spread across my face content to pretend that I'm just a normal person not writing royalty with bodyguards stationed at her door. 'Do you think that we could actually get away with it?' I ask him considering the plan we had just concocted. 'They work for you.' he reminds me before brushing a kiss across my forehead, 'If you want to go on a date it shouldn't be a media sanctioned event.'

'Our privacy,' he continues, 'your privacy is a high priority.' Entwining my fingers through his, my smile widens, 'You had it right the first-time camera boy. Our privacy. Yours's, mine, Clarity's and anyone else we come into contact with shouldn't be gossip for the world over their morning coffee. If that means drip feeding information to the media, then so be it.'

A knock on the door shatters the golden peace our bubble created for me. My doctor pokes his head into the room wearing a smile, 'It's time. Are you sure you want to go out the front? The parking lot is six-foot-deep in media crews.' 'She's not going out the front.' Josh all but growls at him. 'Or the back.' My new body guard steps inside the door, 'That's also under siege. How comfortable are you with the unconventional Miss la Croix?'

The unconventional being a body bag on a cart and a ride in the back of the morgue wagon. Weirdly, it turns out that I'm extremely comfortable with this mode of transport if it means that I can slip past the cameras unnoticed. 'I think your both going to have to share the bag.' He eyes us both sizing up the bag against our combined girth, 'Or not.' Josh unzips his backpack, 'I had a feeling I would need a disguise.' His hand dips into the cavernous space only to appear holding his camera and a faded blue baseball cap signed by Oliver Green. 'A lot of the piranhas out there actually looked up to the guy. Most of them are still carrying the same gear as he does.' He takes one of my shaking hands between both of his, 'Baby trust me this will work. We are going to get out of here. No one will know we've left the building.'

He helps me into the body bag laying on the cart and zips me in himself. 'You've got to play at being a statue.' Geoff reminds me right before I lose sight of Josh's face. A few minutes pass and then the cart begins to move. The whole experience very surreal. The roar of the crowd penetrates through the thin material of the bag. 'Lie still.' Geoff reminds me through clenched teeth, 'Don't take deep breaths.' Jostling our way through the crowd I feel the zipper start moving. 'Oi don't you have any respect for the dead you wanker!' Geoff is beside my head in an instant re zipping the bag probably giving the person who touched me his trade mark 'made of stone' look. Less than three seconds later and the crowd miraculously parts to let us through.

Two days have passed and I'm feeling trapped. The whole princess locked in the tower thing is starting to bug the hell out of me. Pressing speed dial on my phone I count the rings. One. Two. He always picks up after two. I think Josh is paranoid that every time I call I could be in trouble.

'Hi Princess.' The warmth of his voice washes over me calming me instantly. 'I was wondering if you could meet me for lunch today?' My nerves peek back out. Ugh. when was the last time I was this formal around Josh? 'I'm not being lured to a shotgun wedding, am I? Do I need to wear a suit?'

(Josh)

'No.' laughter breaks the tension in her voice, 'But I do need to see you today.'

Checking my schedule, I smile knowing she can't see how happy I am. Clarity has an overnight play date leaving me free. 'I can do lunch.' Her laughter spills over at my formal reply. Formal isn't who we are. Not with each other. 'Good I'll cook your favourites.' Cook. Her place. My mind wanders a little. 'Josh.' I sense she's been saying my name for a couple of minutes. 'Yeah.' I manage. 'Want to drive the Shelby?' she asks. 'I want to do more than just drive your car.' My brain explodes, 'I'm finally going to see your room.'

Her home as she so casually calls it is a freaking palace. Forget mansion. She may live in the same gated community as all the other high rollers in our city but she definitely owns the whole place. I half expect someone to come out and yell at me for walking on the lawn in three different languages and be met at the door by a snooty butler. Instead, I'm met by her smiling face. A smile that doesn't quite reach her eyes. I see the bruises around them that her light makeup can't quite conceal. 'So, no butler?' I ask stepping across the thresh hold into a staged interior. 'I have problems with other people constantly fawning over me in my private time.' She shut the huge oak door behind her.

'Follow me.' she catches hold of my hand, 'It's a big place.' Yeah. This place is definitely staged. Too perfect. Too balanced. No personal belongings or photos anywhere. 'Doesn't feel right.' I mutter half under my breath until she shows me through a double set of sliding barn doors into a mini apartment. 'Let me guess, 'I say dryly noticing all the personal touches, 'Your bedroom is in the turret.'

(Millie)

'Actually,' I reply with the straightest face I can muster, 'yes, it is.' I insisted on it but he doesn't need to know that. No need for him to add to that 'princess in a tower' crap he's got stuck in his head right now. I head to the back of the apartment to check on the spaghetti sauce I've got simmering away on the stove before showing him the rest of my personal space. In such a huge home I only occupy six rooms. Seven if you include the indoor pool/gym area. 'Sweetheart.' something in his voice makes me look up at him, 'You're stalling. No expectations remember?' I study his face for a moment before nodding. 'Breathe.' He encourages me, 'I don't have to see it.' I almost miss the gleam in his eyes daring me to rise to his bait. 'I've never had anyone in here but my mother.' He twists the knob on the door and steps into my refuge from the world.

(Josh)

I expect something girly instead I find the refined French country theme of the apartment has been carried through into her private rooms. I never noticed how many different shades of white there was until now. Each blending with the other seamlessly against the oak flooring and matching timber furniture. Her bed head looks as comfortable as the overstuffed reading chair and oversized foot rest beside it. Floor to ceiling windows overlooks the back garden.

In my defence, Cassie's taking interior design and constantly leaves her magazines in our apartment. 'It's beautiful just like the woman who lives in it.' She smiles mysteriously before opening the door to her ensuite bathroom. 'There's a chandelier in your bathroom baby!' I dramatically clutch at my chest acting as badly as I can so she knows I'm kidding, 'Now I know I've died and gone to the land of the rich and infamous.' A suppressed giggle reaches my ears just as her delicate hand touches my arm. 'I have to check on the sauce and then I need to fill you in on my schedule for the next few weeks.' Her words do nothing to reassure me.

'I'm going to an in-house therapy place.' She's worried about how I'll take the news, 'I think I'll have maybe two weeks break and then the book tour will start straight after that.' 'What haven't you been telling me?' I grab onto the tailcoats of my last shreds of patience and hang onto them for grim life. 'Nightmares. Raging nightmares with screaming and night sweats.' She twists her fingers together. Anxiety levels rising. 'They're not going away and I need to get help. I can't...I won't live the rest of my life from the bubble of my bedroom afraid that someone is going to do something horrible to me again.'

(Millie)

He takes a moment to himself staring out at my garden. Processing everything I've said to him. Tiptoeing out of the room I leave him to it while I finish making lunch.

'I'm sorry.' He drops a kiss on my forehead. 'Nothing to be sorry about.' I say while serving the pasta. Bypassing the table, I seat myself on one of the couches. Josh eyes the food on the coffee table in front of us. 'Why didn't you tell me it was happening?' He persists as he reaches for a bowl. 'Because you have exams coming. Because Jed is sick and needs you.' Accepting the bowl of food, he places in my hands I added softly, 'Because I can't always be the damsel in distress that needs rescuing.'

'No but you can tell me that something is going on, so I don't feel like I'm the last one to know.' He pointed out reasonably. 'I'm going to make mistakes.' I admit softly, 'You're my first boyfriend.' Hearing a choking sound, I raise my eyes off my food. 'I left conventional school at 13.' I point out handing him a glass of water, 'I missed most of your usual high school experience. Boyfriends. Parties. Dates. You could say I've had a lot of firsts lately.'

We finish our food in comfortable silence. 'Come on.' He sweeps me off my feet easily holding me bridal style. He strides easily through my house and deposits me on my turned down bed. 'You haven't been sleeping well.' He states tucking me in like a small child before getting comfortable on the other side on top of the covers. He wraps an arm around me and pulls me close. 'Close your eyes Amelie.'

It was those tender moments that kept me going during the three weeks I spent at the rehab hotel for broken down celebrities. The generic name of Hope Springs really didn't encompass the purpose behind the facility. They took away all my phone, my watch, my iPad and my laptop.

Missing you

Missing you more

I didn't get a chance to say goodbye before I left.

My flight had left so early that I hadn't wanted to wake him up. He had stayed the entire night holding me in his arms to chase my nightmares away. I had had to scribble him a quick note that let him know what day I would be home.

Do you want to say still goodbye?

Who was it? Julie? Debbie? Sue?

I'll murder the lot of them :X

Don't go all Pirates of the Caribbean on me writer girl.

My heart couldn't take you being in danger again so soon.

They hadn't managed to scare him off. Grinning like a Cheshire cat I typed my next few texts hoping that his schedule was clear.

Can you meet me tonight?

Corner of James and 25th in an hour.

Can you come?

Can I bring a camera? Oh shit. I have Clarity tonight.

I promised you a photo on our first date :) Bring her too. I miss hanging out with her. What I've got in mind is family friendly.

We'll be there baby.

Anything I need to know?

I was under strict house arrest. My fans knew I was seeing someone new but there were no photos of Josh and I together yet. Sue had said that Lily couldn't see her boyfriend. She didn't say that Amelie St. James couldn't have a private moment from the world.

I may be sneaking out to see you.

Sue has me under house arrest.

Dress fancy-ish. Expect Millie.

(Josh)

Be safe Princess.

Finally, she had access to her phone again. 'She's back isn't she.' Jed raised his head off his pillow. 'Yeah.' I rubbed the back of my neck, 'I've got a date tonight. Are you going to be okay without me or Dad around?' He shook his head, 'Call Norah.' Norah's lawyer had gotten her off on a technicality. She had been forced to dry out in prison. Unwilling to let Jed's memories be tainted of us fighting all the time we had a tentative agreement in place that she was at the house for him and him alone. Never when Clarity was home and never with my Mother in tow. I did as he asked and relayed the message that he wanted to spend a few hours with her alone. 'Take the charger.' Jed raised himself painfully up on one arm to study my face. *Take the charger*. 'You're not going anywhere yet.' I pause in front of him holding my one good working outfit. She had said fancy-ish not red carpet.

'The charger's classy.' he shrugged his other shoulder, 'Your Ford wouldn't make the trip. I was listening to the engine. Needs work. Car seat's already in it. Better get moving if you have to wrestle with the little monkey.' He scoops the keys off the bedside table and tosses them at me. He fell gently back against the pillows and picked up the tv remote.

Since he's moved in I don't recognise my room anymore. A lot of my posters and belongings were packed away almost overnight. We're not the same people who grew up sharing it. 'You're going to be late lover boy.' He throws a dirty sock at me. Some things never change.

I sit on the hood of the car enjoying the hustle and bustle of the city around me Clarity's asleep in her car seat. 'Nice car.' Amelie's voice breaks me out of my reverie. 'You look amazing.' She's showing off her legs under a white sundress paired with a denim jacket with a denim bag and brown sandals. On anyone else the outfit would be considered casual. On her it looks a million bucks.

(Millie)

'So do you.' The response passes my lips without filtering. They are temporarily disabled by how hot he looks in his black trousers and black dress shirt. In his arms, Clarity is dressed in a Disney princess dress with fairy wings. 'She couldn't decide between princess or fairy so we're being both today.' he shrugs leaning forward brushing his lips over mine before declaring, 'We missed you.' 'I missed you both too.' Scooping Clarity out of his arms I twirl her around listening to her laugh. 'Where are we going tonight?' He takes the opportunity to kiss me properly keeping us steady with his hand placed in the small of my back. 'How does a movie under the stars sound?' I ask breathlessly. 'Like a drive in?' he clarifies. 'No, a movie in the park. Bring your own everything. It starts at 7.30. I think they're showing the first of the Star Wars prequels tonight.' He opens the passenger door and helps me inside before strapping Clarity into her seat with a five-point harness.

I love the Star Wars movies. Even the 'princess' is quite capable of fighting for herself and does so most of the time. The park is some ways into the suburbs. Along the way we buy dinner to go, a couple of picnic blankets and some readymade sweet n salty popcorn to share. Picking our way through the dark we set up just as *'A long time ago, in a galaxy far far away...'* rolls up the screen. 'Come here.' he whispers in my ear. Rearranging me so that I'm leaning my back against his chest and Clarity is snuggled up in my lap. Josh covers us both with the second blanket. He holds his camera out in front of us and takes a selfie in the dark. 'Will it turn out?' I ask softly in his ear as he checks his work. 'I'll show you how good I am when I drop you home princess.' the self-assured smirk is back in his voice again.

Sneaking me home has never been so much fun. My phone rings the minute I get inside the house from the garage where I left Josh professing his undying love to my car collection. 'Sue, what can I do for you at this hour.' Placing Clarity down in the crib I had set up in the nursery I had created. I exit the room swiftly leaving the door open a crack and making sure the monitor was switched on. 'You went out Lily.' she states bluntly, 'Josh was seen bringing you home a few minutes ago.' 'Was I in the car? Did your spies tell you if he was alone or not?' Calmly I fill the kettle and begin to make some hot chocolate.

'They said Josh.' she admits uncertainly. 'You said I couldn't go out.' I

point out reasonably, 'You didn't say he couldn't come over. Goodnight Sue.'
Placing my phone on the counter in front of me I continue to work until his arms encircle me from behind.

CHAPTER EIGHTEEN

Mamma drama karma

(Josh)

I woke up completely relaxed the next morning. The heavy scent of coffee permeated the apartment and Amelie's soft voice was singing completely out of tune to Alex & Sierra's 'I love You'. Moving swiftly, I took the opportunity to nuzzle her bare neck before replying, 'I love you too baby but you won't have a singing career anytime soon.'

She handed me a mug of freshly brewed coffee before popping a slice of banana in her mouth. Carrying the breakfast tray to the table I watch her swallow her mouthful. 'How did your exams go?' she asks with a smile. 'I think I'll get good grades.' Grades? Who talks school first thing in the morning? Especially the morning after such a great night. She blushes, 'You mumbled that aloud.' Taking a bite of plain toast, I ask innocently, 'What did I say, princess?'

The sound of her phone ringing interrupts what she was about to say to me. 'Thank you.' She ends the call swiftly and pops another piece of fruit into her mouth. Her face is too innocent. 'I can spend the day out of the palace.' She finally reveals. 'I'm watching Jed later and Clarity has a play date. Want to come with?'

There's an unfamiliar car parked outside the house when we arrive. Out of the corner of my eye, I see my beautiful girl turn white. 'It could just be someone getting after hours help on their coursework from Dad.' She nods her head uncertainly in agreement as I pull on the hand brake. 'Or not.' I add silently to myself as I see my mother stalk across the lawn towards us. 'Stay here.' I tell Amelie before unfolding myself out the driver's door and shutting it behind me.

'You aren't welcome here.' Folding my arms, I make sure that I've angled myself so that she can't see Amelie. 'You had me locked up for something I didn't do.' she shouts stabbing her finger into my chest. Shouting could turn into screaming real fast if she wasn't appeased. I check over my shoulder to see Amelie on her phone. 'I've come for Clarity.' Her demands are met with my best bored stare. Dad appears on the porch his voice calm, 'It's Saturday Ginny.'

'I've come for Clarity.' She repeats to him before adding furiously, 'You look at me when I'm talking to you son.' 'You walked out on me and Dad. Took my chance to know my baby girl away from me when you pushed Jed and Norah together. I don't acknowledge any relationship with you. Like Dad says it's Saturday. My time. Clarity's out at the moment.' Pointing out the obvious to the woman in front of me I add, 'Jed needs to rest and Norah's off the clock. Clarity's got all her parents right here.'

'If you keep causing a public disturbance I'll send you back.' Dad speaks again mobile phone in hand, 'I won't let you come into my home unless you calm down Guinevere.' Her fury subsides into cold anger. Slamming her hand down on the bonnet of the car, 'You are going to regret your actions.' 'I'm not afraid of you.' Staring her down I'm surprised to feel Amelie's small hand wrap around the one I have behind my back.

(Millie)

Squeezing his hand tightly I exit the car quietly behind him. 'Jed is dying.' Stepping out from behind Josh I eye his mother curiously. I don't understand why she wants Clarity so badly. I do know I'm only seeing a few of the dysfunctional dynamics of this family. I don't care. 'Ginny was it?' I ask politely before adding, 'I'm Lily la Croix. Josh's girlfriend.'

I've seen the transitioning looks so many times that they're the reason I have trust issues. Her anger turns into confusion followed by avarice. Greed on steroids. 'Lovely to meet you.' I lie through my teeth before adding sweetly, 'I'm sure you understand why everyone is a little on edge at the moment.' Her whole demeanour changes and she drops the tough act. 'They said he had a famous girlfriend. They didn't tell me it was you.' She's quietly calculating how much my outfit is worth. 'I'm not going to write you any cheques.' I state bluntly and add now that I have her attention, 'Jed is going to need the support of his whole family if he has any chance of fighting this cancer. Tearing into Josh, demanding he hand his daughter over to you and threatening us isn't helping. Your only choice is to go away and calm down properly. Find a time that suits Jed's energy levels and come back then. Be his mum because he needs you now more than ever.'

I want to add the words 'can you do that' but I don't want to provoke her into losing her temper again. The heavy weight of Josh's arm settles along the back of my shoulders sweeping me into his side. He presses a soft kiss to my temple and says quietly, 'Go and tell Jed not to get up.' Giving Ginny a wide berth I make it to the porch where Professor Patterson is waiting. 'You did good Lily.' He says eyes not straying from his unhinged ex-wife.

Inside I find Norah perching uncomfortably in the overstuffed armchair that has been pulled up beside Jed's bed. I hear her voice trying to convince him to stay resting. 'The Professor and Josh both told me to tell you to stay put.' I feel uncomfortable being in their presence without someone to protect me. Norah flies out of the chair and pulls me into a clingy hug. Helpless I look at Jed for an explanation. 'She's a bit emotional at the moment.' He lifts one shoulder in a shrug. Norah's heavy Barbie make up resembles the stage make up for KISS. 'Come on.' Pushing her towards the bathroom I eye Jed sternly, 'Try and get comfortable again.' I

can tell he's exhausted when he doesn't
argue with me.

Grabbing my packet of face wipes
out of my tote I use them to bring out the
real Norah underneath all the war paint she's
been using to hide from the world. 'They
rounded me up too.' She admits and asks
quietly, 'Why are you being so nice to us?'
'Because no matter what you do right now
we're family and family take care of each
other.' The answer rolls off my tongue
without hesitation adding, 'You've raised a
pretty amazing little girl. Oliver knew all
about her. The cops wouldn't have been
doing their job if they didn't check out all
the threats. I'm sorry if you hate me for it.
Keeping her identity anonymous for as long
as I can is a huge priority for me.'

She hugs me again before looking at
herself in the mirror, 'We've spent so long
putting up walls just to survive. I'm not used
to this.' Giving me a small smile, she adds,
'You're alright Millie, Lily or whatever
name you're going by today.' I recognise
this for what it is. A bonding moment. A

moment in which truths are revealed. 'Lily is my alias for work. Millie was an alias for when I was living on campus.' Looking straight at her so she would know that I was speaking the truth, 'My name is Amelie. You can call me that if you'd like.'

'Amelie St. James!' Josh's roar echoes throughout the basement. Norah smirks, 'I know that tone. Good luck. It's been nice knowing the real you Amelie St. James.' She saunters out of the bathroom and tells Josh I'm just washing my hands. Traitor.

His whole countenance has darkened with anger. 'Stalling won't make this conversation disappear sweetheart.' He leans against the door post blocking the way out. 'She calmed down.' I say in a small voice before sitting on the edge of the bath tub. I have no defence. He knows it. 'She could have hurt you.' He grinds out, 'Do I have to arrange extra security for while you're away?' Low blow. I would never be so stupid. Not while I was working.

'I'd take you, Ryan and Cassie with me but you have Clarity. School. Jed.' My words are barely audible. He squats down on the floor in front of me. 'Her unsaid words were hurting you.' My mouth runs away from me, 'I couldn't just sit there Josh. I love you. I wanted to protect you from her.' He crooks a finger under my chin bringing my eyes level with his. 'Say that again.' He demands softly. Swallowing reflexively, I repeat, 'I wanted to protect you from her?' He laughs. The sound is low and my heart responds to it with a crazy rhythm. 'Not that bit.'

'I couldn't just sit there Josh. I love…oh!' I had basically declared my love for him without realising it. Blushing I repeat the words he wants to hear over again, 'I love you.' 'I love you too.' His eyes have lightened in colour, 'Please will you wait in the car next time? Trust me to deal with the problem. If I need you to move, I'll tell you.' Leaning my forehead against his I whisper, 'Only if you don't treat me like a piece of china.

' 'I can't hear what they're saying to each other.' Jed complains from the next room, 'If you're going to have the lives of a soap opera at least be loud enough for us to enjoy it.' Josh laughs softly before pulling me close. 'Can't you tell he's kissing the girl?' Norah chides. By the sounds coming from them, they're doing a little kissing themselves.

CHAPTER NINETEEN

Greatest show

He's aiming a camera up at the iron girders in the building structure concentrating on getting the best angle. Completely engrossed in his work, he does not realise he isn't alone until I lock the door of the Creative Arts Building behind me.

'I didn't know anyone was in there.' He calls out pointing his camera at the ground. Last time we were in this situation he had thought nothing of aiming it at my face and taking an intrusive photo. Flipping my hair back over my shoulder I smile, 'I'm not just anyone camera boy.' His hands tremble slightly. I meant this as a good surprise. We haven't seen each other since I began the book tour.

'I've dreamt of this moment so much I don't know if I should trust my eyes writer girl.' He puts the camera down carefully before stepping up to examine my face. Sweeping me into a hug he kisses my earlobe, 'Hello Amelie.' He sweeps my hair further away from the back of my neck to reveal the tiny hummingbird tattoo I acquired in Ireland. He looks better than I remember. The photos we took together didn't capture his true personality. The way he makes me shiver and the fact that he knows how good he is at doing it.

'Very delicate Amelie.' He murmurs close to my ear, 'Are there any more?' Smiling wickedly, I slide the waist band of my jeans down a little to reveal the top part of a compass. 'I definitely want to see the rest of that when we get home.' He spins me around in his arms. 'Anything else I should know about?'

'I may or may not have a J somewhere on my body.' Biting my lip, I watch the warring emotions on his face. He wants to throw me over his shoulder and drag me home to bed to play hunt the tattoo. He also wants to make this memorable since this tour is only one month in. In the end he compromises, 'If I take you out for drinks at the Lakeside Village Tavern will you please show me?'

We fit together. It didn't matter how weird my life is or normal his was. Together we were camera boy and writer girl. Our world revolved around us in that moment and life was good.

That was four years ago…

If someone had told me that in my moments of madness I would meet my future family I would have laughed. Josh held on. He endured the weird, went along with the wonderful and picked me up when I cried from sheer exhaustion. He insisted I started keeping better hours and made sure that I ate properly. Everything clicked into place when Jed died. He held on for another two years helping Clarity cement her relationship with Josh. Norah signed her completely into Josh's custody. Suddenly we were completely responsible for a five-year-old whose whole world had been tipped on its axis.

'We're just about there Miss la Croix.' My body guard startled me out of my memories of the past. A small smile graced my face as my limo pulled into the queue approaching yet another red-carpet event. Only this time the world would be in for quite a surprise. My phone vibrated inside my clutch. Checking my messages my smile grew wider.

Ready baby?

Showtime Camera boy.

I couldn't believe that I had been given free tickets to attend the Oscars. Directors and producers were willing to do just about anything to get me to sign a contract for Lilac Cove. Sliding out gracefully, I bent my head and held out my hand, 'Ready to meet the world sweetheart? Everyone's waiting to meet you.' Clarity took my hand without hesitation. The world grew quiet as it held its collective breath. She looked completely adorable in her fancy dress. 'Lily!' reporters began to vie for my attention. Gliding over the carpet gracefully I made small talk with entertainment tonight before they asked the question everyone wanted an answer for, 'Lily who is with you tonight and who is her designer?' 'This is my daughter Clarity Patterson. She is wearing a dress made by her Grandfather for the occasion.' 'Oh my. the shocks keep coming tonight on the red carpet. See you after the break.' Waiting for the camera man to count her out I smile at him, 'See Clarity, I told you Daddy would be at the show.'

Josh hands the camera off to his offsider and smooths down his tuxedo. 'How are my two best girls?' The reporter's mouth is opening and closing resembling a goldfish. 'Yes, you can have an exclusive. Not tonight. Contact my agent.' I promise her turning us around just as she's being counted back in for her next segment. Picking Clarity up in his arm right arm, Josh wraps his left one around my shoulders guiding us towards the entry way. 'Who's next?' he asks out of the side of his mouth keeping his smile firm dazzling the public. 'Lily la Croix?' A masculine voice interrupts our deliberation. Turning I'm suddenly face to face with my dream pick for the lead male role. 'This is my husband Joshua and our daughter Clarity.' determined not to leave them out while I was busy making connections and promoting dreams of something bigger than the books I had written.

'I was wondering if I could have a photo with you.' he admits with a charming smile. Handing the mobile to Josh who immediately checks the lighting and angle options we pose together. 'I'm looking forward to working with you.' he admits and adds, 'You have a beautiful family.' 'This role was written especially for you.' I smile and take the phone back from Josh checking the shot before handing it over, 'I can't wait to see how you bring it to life.'

Inwardly I'm literally fan girling. He waits until we're alone before whispering in my ear. 'Hold it together until we get home baby.' Josh smiles down at me, 'Is it everything you dreamed of?' Tilting my head to one side enjoying the moment I take a look around at our illustrious company in the theatre, 'More.'

Song List

Freaks-Timmy Trumpet, Savage
Beautifully Unfinished-Ella Henderson
Monsters-Ruelle
Demons-Imagine Dragons
Backbone-Daughtry
Broken-Seether, Amy Lee
Amnesia-5 Seconds of Summer
Thunder-Imagine Dragons
Havana-Pentatonix
Stand inside your love-Eowyn
This is me/Scars to your beautiful-Joey Stamper
Roses and Violets-Alexander Jean
Gold Digger-Glee Cast version
You Don't Own Me-Grace, G-Easy
It's Goin Down-Descendants 2 soundtrack
Worth the Fight-Cimorelli
Starships-Pentatonix
We Are Young-Pentatonix
Independent Woman part 1-Destiny's Child
Granted-Josh Groban
Heart is a Weapon-Walk Off the Earth
Wake Me Up When September Ends-Green Day
Little Girl-Christine Grimmie
My Demons-Starset
Who You Are-Jessie J
The Man Who Can't Be Moved-The Script
It's All Coming Back to Me Now- Celine Dion
Gladiator-The Girl and The Dreamcatcher

Let It Be-The Beatles
Written in the Stars-The Girl and The Dreamcatcher
I Love You-Alex & Sierra
Coming Home-Keith Urban, Julia Michaels
Skin-Sixx am
You Are The Reason-Calum Scott
The Greatest Show-The Greatest Show soundtrack

I dreamed a dream...

This novella is being released in conjunction with the first Story Tellers Festival in Raymond Terrace. Everyone has a story to tell and everyone tells their story in a slightly different way. Writing is such a solitary occupation that unless we actively go looking for a group to belong to we are often bereft of our own tribe. The wheels in my mind started turning and I wanted to organise an event that would not only bring my tribe together uniting the writers in my area but also the other creative branches.

What if we all got together and celebrated creativity itself? Somewhere where we could go to network and access businesses or services. Somewhere where we could advertise and promote our current products. Somewhere where we could hold workshops and artisan markets. This dream is coming to fruition. For more information on further events go to the Facebook page: @StoryTellersRTNSW

About the Author

Author of Millie or Lily which is being released to celebrate the first Story Tellers Festival in Raymond Terrace. She is also the author of the Elanna's Children series. Her Wattpad books include When I Made You Smile and The Phoenix Sisters-History. An advocate for greater inclusivity in the wider community Ms Wright injects her characters with realistic quirks her readers can relate to.

Past achievements include running a local writers' group out of Port Stephens Library-Raymond Terrace Branch, working with Irrawang High School in their Blue

Ribbon Author mentoring project and being published in five countries with her poetry.

Ms Wright lives and works out of her home in Raymond Terrace, New South Wales Australia. She enjoys spending time with her family, is a Gryffindor, chocoholic, constantly stows away on the TARDIS and owns a cat who likes to keep to a routine.

Social Media Links

Website: www.buttakittin.wix.com/mysite

Facebook: @elanna11children11

Twitter: @MJWright1976

Instagram: elanna11children11

Wattpad:

https://www.wattpad.com/user/Elanna11Chi
ldren11